In Love With The King of Chicago 2

AJ Dix

TEXT UCP TO 22828 TO SUBSCRIBE TO OUR MAILING LIST

If you would like to join our team, submit the first 3-4 chapters of your completed manuscript to

Submissions@UrbanChapterspublications.com

Acknowledgements:

I want to start off by thanking you all for the support of this release. I spent a lot of sleepless nights working on this, so it'll be better than the first, and I hope I delivered!

Thank you, Jah, and the rest of my UCP family for your constant support and encouragement; especially Brii and Dee Ann who always get me together when I'm doubting myself. I appreciate you ladies soooo much.

Hope you all enjoy, and don't forget to leave reviews!

Where we left off...

Karter

    I had officially been Mrs. Wright for three months now, and I was on cloud nine. I agreed to clear Big Mama's house out and rent it out. Dez had people come and do some work on the house, and I was on my way to go see the finished product. When I pulled up, I saw my mother sitting on the porch, and she had a black eye that looked fresh. It wasn't really cold at the end of March, but it was definitely too cold to just be sitting on the porch.

    "How long have you been sitting out here? And what happened to your eye?"

    "I been here all night. I didn't know you moved out, I was waiting and hoping you stopped by."

    "Ok, so what happened to your eye?"

    "Your father, he—"

    "That's not my father."

    "Well Kevin, he beat my ass because I wouldn't agree to set you and your boyfriend up. He started smoking more, and he lost all our money gambling. He said your guy looked like he had money, and he wanted to rob him."

    "Well, first of all, my HUSBAND would kill you and him if you even thought about it, and so would I. So, I advise you to leave, like now."

"I told him I wouldn't do it, and he snapped. I really came back to build a relationship with you. I'm sorry I let a man keep me away from you so long, but please Karter, you have to forgive me."

"I don't have to do shit but stay black and die. You really have to go; do you need some money?"

"I didn't come here for that, I don't want your money."

"Well, that's all I got for you, so here." I reached in and grabbed all the cash I had in my purse. "This should be enough to get you a room or a bus ticket, but don't come back here."

I walked past her and went into the house, making sure I locked the door behind me. When I looked around at Big Mama's house, completely empty, I broke down a little. I couldn't believe I was actually doing this. I always said I was never leaving this house. I was doing a full background and credit check on whoever I rented to because if they messed this house up, I was going to be in jail for a homicide.

I wiped my tears and did my walkthrough of the house. I can't lie, this shit was nice. I was thinking about changing my mind again, but I didn't wanna hear Dezmund's mouth. When I left out, thankfully, my mother was gone, so I got into the car and headed to the studio for practice with the Divas.

I had a lot of new girls on both squads, and I was happy that people liked us enough to want to join the family.

There weren't any competitions I was signing us up for anytime soon, because I needed all of girls to be in sync with each other.

We worked on two stands that took us almost four hours to get right. I called Dez after I dismissed all the girls, because he hated when I left out alone when it was dark.

"I'm pulling up now, baby."

"Ok."

I grabbed my bag and waited for him to knock on the door before I came out.

"You look tired as hell, bae."

"I am tired; you know I been running around, and I went to go look at the house."

He walked me around the building where my car was parked, and someone jumped out from behind the dumpster and scared me. Dez pulled me behind him, and the masked man was holding a gun to him.

"Give me your money!"

"Nigga, I ain't got no cash on me, fuck I look like?"

"Give me that watch then."

"Yeah, you can have it, I hope you let God see it too, bro."

Dez started playing with his watch, and I saw the gun that was tucked behind his back. I snatched it out and shot through the space Dez had between his arm. I wasn't looking, so I didn't even know if I shot him until I heard his body drop, and some groaning.

"Good shit, bae. Next time, Imma need you to have your eyes open when you shoot."

He walked up to the man and bent down to take the mask off.

"Ain't this yo pops, bae?" I didn't say anything as I just stared at Kevin's chest move up and down slowly. I heard some sirens, and Dez stood up and dusted his pants off.

"Karter, come on, we gotta go."

"Did I... did I kill 'im?"

"It was either him or me, baby, but we can't sit here and discuss this shit right now."

My ears were still ringing from the gunshot, and my head was spinning. I just knew I was going to pass out, until Dez grabbed my arm and had to basically drag me to the car. I was still holding the smoking gun as Dez drove like a bat outta hell. I didn't think I would get that visual of that body hitting the ground out of my head. I never even shot a gun before.

'God, I hope I don't get punished for this.'

"Shit!"

"What?"

I snapped out of my trance to see blue lights flashing behind us. I started to panic, but Dez took the gun and stashed it in a secret compartment that was in the dash.

"Just relax, bae. I'll take care of this, it's probably because I was speeding."

I saw his lips moving, but I couldn't hear anything over the sound of my racing heart.

Dez rolled the window down halfway as one officer came to his window, and another was on the passenger side flashing his light in my face.

"License, registration, and proof of insurance, please?"

"What am I being stopped for, Officer?"

"You were going 80 in a 65, sir."

"Aite bro, I gotta reach in the glove compartment."

"Move slowly." The officer had his hand on his gun, and my eyes got big as I watched his every move. With all the shit going on with police killing black people, males especially, I feared for Dez's life as well as my own.

Dez handed over his documents, and the officers walked back to their car. Five minutes later, another squad car pulled up, and Dez cursed under his breath as they approached the car again. This time, the officer tapped on my window.

"Ma'am, do you have identification?"

"What you need her shit for? I'm the one driving, you pulled me over for speeding, right? Fuck outta here with that shit."

"Babe, it's ok, calm down." I got my license and handed it to the officer. He stepped back and said

something into his walkie talkie before he came back to my window.

"Ma'am, I need you to step out and put your hands behind your back."

"Karter, don't get yo ass out this car." Dez rolled my window back up, and the officer snatched at the door handle. I didn't know what to do as I felt the urge to throw up all over the place.

"You bet not fuck my door up while you snatching on my shit." The officer put his hand on his gun, but this time, he pulled it out and had it pointing at me.

"Open the door and step out, NOW!"

"Get your fucking gun out my wife face, bitch." Dez hopped out the car and sprinted around the car, and I got out too so I could stop him from doing something crazy.

"Dezmund, NO! Get back in the car, please, just get back in the car." The officer grabbed my arm and threw me against the car, and the next thing I knew, Dez punched him in the face and he hit the ground. Another squad car pulled up, and I tried to grab my phone off the seat so I could call Melodee or Dame, or anybody.

"PUT YOUR HANDS UP, NOW!"

We now had five guns drawn on us, and Dez just gave me a hug and kissed me on the lips.

"Don't say shit, whatever they ask you, ok? You. Don't. Know. Shit." I shook my head up and down, and he gave me a kiss on the lips.

Dez put his hands up and got down on his knees, so I did the same thing.

He was tackled first and put into handcuffs, then they grabbed me. As I was put into the back of a police car, I was crying my eyes out. When we made it to the station, I was put in a cold room and handcuffed to a chair. I think I was sitting there for an hour, and the whole time, I heard Dez yelling that they better not have touched me.

A female officer dressed in a pantsuit walked into the room with a file in her hand, and she sat down in front of me.

"Hello, Mrs. Wright. I'm Detective Normal, and I'm investigating the murder of a Ms. Jazmyne Fields."

"What? And what does that have to do with me?"

"We have reason to believe you had something to do with it, or at least know something about it. I'm just trying to get to the bottom of this."

"I don't know anything about that, I didn't even know she was dead. So, you can get me a lawyer if I'm being accused of something so serious."

Here I was, thinking I was arrested for shooting my father, and it was about Jazz. I honestly didn't know she was killed. I wondered if Dez had something to do with that.

"Is that your final answer?"

"Yes, it is. I'll take lawyer for eight hundred, Alex."

"Ok, I see we have a regular old comedian on our hands. Take a look at these pictures and I'll be back."

She left out the room and left me sitting in the room by myself. I looked down at the pictures, and they were of Jazz laying on the floor with blood all over the front of her shirt. I pushed the pictures onto the floor.

Another detective came in and sat in the same chair Detective Normal was previously in.

"How are you, Mrs. Wright?"

"I'll be fine when I can get out of here. Can I get my phone call, please?"

"Yeah, I can help you out if you can help me out."

"I don't know how I can help you, sir. Where is my husband?"

"Your husband is fine; it's you I'm worried about. Do you know how serious it is to be looked at for a homicide? It's looking premeditated in the eyes of the law. If I understand correctly, Ms. Fields had an affair with your husband?"

"Noooo, she didn't have shit with my husband, so you don't understand correctly, obviously."

"We have a witness that says you two got into an altercation at your husband's club the day before she got killed; is that correct?"

"Well, I don't know when she got killed, but I could've sworn I asked for a lawyer. Why are you even in here?" He gave me slick smile and stood up out the chair.

"We'll be back with you shortly."

After what felt like an eternity of sitting in this room alone, I started to get pissed, and I had to pee. All I could think about was Dez, and that they were going to do something to him. I hadn't heard his voice in an hour, and I was wondering if he was even still in the precinct.

"HEELLLLLOOOOOO!! I NEED TO GO TO THE BATHROOM! CAN ANYBODY HEAR ME?" I started banging on the table with my free hand, and someone finally opened the door.

"Can I help you?" This six-foot lady came in here with an attitude, like I wanted to be in here.

"Somebody need to help me, I have to use the bathroom. I been sitting here for hours, when can I make my phone call? And where the hell is my husband and my lawyer, for the 50*th* time? I'm going to sue the shit out of the city."

"They actually told me to come let you go, so come on, you can follow me. But, make sure you keep your phone on, and don't leave the country anytime soon." She unlocked the cuffs, and I had to move my hands around to get feeling back in them. I stood up to walk in front of her when she gently grabbed my arm.

"Ma'am, did you get hurt?"

"No, why?"

"There's blood on your pants."

I looked down, and sure enough, there was blood between my legs. I didn't know what the hell was going on because I had my period already, at least I thought I did. I actually couldn't remember the last time I had my period.

"Oh my God, I need to get to a hospital." I ran out the room and saw Dame and Melodee standing in the waiting room looking pissed.

"Mel, take me to the hospital, where is Dez? Has he come out already?"

"They not tryna let him go, talking about because he assaulted a police officer. What happened, did they hurt you?"

"No, I'm bleeding. What do you mean they're not letting him go? They can't just hold him here, can they? The officer had thrown me against the car, and y'all know how Dez gets."

"Our lawyer is here. He'll be straight, sis. Let's go get you checked out to make sure you're ok."

Melodee pulled me out the door, and Dame was trailing right behind us. She got in the backseat with me, and I started to cry in my lap.

"What if I'm losing another baby, Mel? Now, my husband is in jail and they think I killed Jazz. My life is going from sugar to shit so fast."

"What?!" Dame and Melodee yelled at the same time, and Dame looked back at me with a strange face, like he knew something I didn't.

"When did she get killed?"

"I don't know, I thought the bitch just finally found her some business. They said the day after I whooped her ass in the club, but I didn't do the shit."

"Just relax, we know you're innocent. They don't have any evidence, that's why they couldn't hold you in there."

Dame's phone rang and he handed it to me.

"Here, it's bro."

15

"Hello?"

"Baby, you good?"

"No, I'm bleeding, Dez. I think I'm losing another baby. I'm so scared. Where are you? Are you ok?"

"Calm down. I'll be there soon, ok?"

"When is soon?"

"I don't know, bae. I can't lie, I might do a little time because I'm about to knock a few more of they asses out up in here."

"Dezmund, stop." I laughed, and he did too.

"I just wanted to hear you laugh. I gotta go, but Imma see you soon. Don't be stressing my baby out in there, aite? I love you, Queen."

"I love you too, King."

Chapter One

Karter

Two Days Later…

It hit me like a tidal wave.
Knew that I was in love with you right away, yeah
Turned all my days into brighter days,
even when people say what we do is not ok.

I sat in our bedroom in the same spot I had been in the last two days, playing Jhene Aiko's *Trip* album on repeat. I still hadn't spoken to my husband since I left the precinct the other night, and I was waiting on his call. Last I heard, he was moved to *Cook County Jail*, and from the stories I heard about it, that was not a place Dez needed to be. Dame kept telling me *don't trip*, but what the hell was I supposed to do knowing my husband was in jail?

Finally deciding to turn my music off, I turned on the TV and tried to find one of my ratchet TV shows to keep me entertained. While I was flipping through the channels, a story on ABC 7 News caught my attention, and I turned the volume all the way up.

"One of our top stories this morning. It was yet another bloody holiday weekend in Chicago. Five more people were shot this morning, bringing the total since Friday afternoon to nearly 50. Twelve people were killed, including an unknown man who was found dead with a gunshot wound to his chest on Chicago's East Side, outside of a popular dance studio."

My phone rang, snapping me out of the trance I was in, and I saw it was Melodee.

"Yes, Mel?" I answered, muting the TV.

"You saw it too huh?"

I sighed and laid back on the bed. My heart broke, seeing the studio surrounded with yellow tape and police officers.

"Has Dame heard anything about Dez yet?"

"No, but he left out a little while ago to see him."

"This is fuckin' stupid. I'm going to see him, I've been waiting too long."

The other line beeped, and it was a call from an unsaved number. "Hold on, Mel."

"Hello?"

"Wassup, bae?" Hearing Dez's husky voice on the other end of the line had me feeling a little relief.

"Dezmund, I swear I was about to be on my way up there. Are you ok? Did they hurt you? When are you coming home?" I fired off each question without taking a breath.

"I'm tryna handle some shit, but trust, you gon' see me soon, baby."

"What are you handling in jail, Dez?" Excuse me if I didn't sound one hundred percent confident, but would you when that person was locked up?

"Do you trust me, Karter?"

"Yes," I answered quickly. It was true, I trusted Dez with my life... but this just seemed crazy.

"Well, trust that your man is taking care of this for us, ok?"

"I just wish you was here."

"Soon baby, I promise. How my baby doing in there? You bet not be stressing and shit, man."

I rubbed my still flat stomach and smiled, thinking of my tiny pea growing inside of me. When I went to the hospital, they informed me that I was nine weeks pregnant, and the bleeding that I experienced was normal.

"How did you know?"

"Dame told me, now how you feelin'?"

"I'm missing my husband, and it sucks— other than that, it's fucking peachy, Dezmund." My voice was breaking as I held in my tears.

"Come on, Bugs, don't cry. It'll be over before you know it. But look, I gotta go. Imma call you again tonight, baby. I love you."

"I love you too."

When I hung the phone up, it felt like a piece of my heart broke. I hated being away from Dez; I just hoped he was serious about seeing me soon.

Beeepp!

The bell at the gate sounded off, and I checked the camera to see who it was. When I saw Melodee, I buzzed the gate and went to the front door to meet her.

Melodee got out the car looking cute, wearing a gray turtleneck sweater, blue jeans, and some gray Uggs. The snow hadn't quite melted yet, so I knew Melodee was gon' wear them boots until summer kicked in.

"Yo ass had me on hold forever, so I had to come check up on you." She handed me a *Cold Stone Creamery* bag, and I wanted to jump all over her.

"I'm sorry. Dez called finally, and I honestly forgot you was on the phone."

"Well damn, I'm hurt." She grabbed her chest, feigning hurt, and I laughed at her.

"Not like that bestie, you know what I mean."

"Nah, I know what you said, but it's cool. You wanna go do something?"

"Like what?"

"I don't know, but it smells depressing in this house and I don't have time to be sad."

"You so irra. I'll go, but Dez is supposed to call me later and I want to be back in the house by then."

"Yeah, yeah — grab yo shit and come on."

I grabbed everything I needed and locked up the house. The fresh air did feel good when I stepped all the way out the house, and I had to thank Melodee for getting me out. If not, I probably would be locked in the house until Dez came home.

Soon, baby.

***

"How this look?" Mel asked, holding up a red sequined top. We ended up at the mall, and Melodee was shopping for the season. I didn't have the desire to buy anything new, especially since I was going to be blowing up soon.

"I think it's cute, and it matches those pumps you bought the other day."

"It wasn't the other day, it was like a few weeks ago. You make it sound like I have a shopping problem."

"I didn't say that, you did." I gave her a knowing look, and we both laughed. I needed this girl time, I was feeling lost in the house by myself. That big ass house felt haunted when I was in it alone.

Chapter Two

Dezmund "Dez"

"I hope you got something good to tell me," I said as I sat down in front of my lawyer and Dame.

"Not quite, even though you're not in the same *business* you were in before; there's still some people with your name at the top of their hit list. Now, they're charging you with assaulting a police officer; if they decide it's a felony, you're looking at three years in prison."

"Fuck that shit!" Dame said hitting the table with his fist.

"Chill, bro." I nodded to my lawyer to continue, and he cleared his throat before he started talking again.

"I can try to convince them to drop it to a misdemeanor, and you'll be looking at a year tops."

"I'm not doing no year away from my family. I suggest you figure something else out, and fast. Got it?"

"Yes, Mr. Wright, I got it. Now, what are we going to do about the murder that's being pinned on your wife?"

"Who's the detective on the case?"

He looked down at the file that was in front of him, "Detective Normal."

Fuck!

I ran my hand down my face and folded my hands on the table in front of me. "Ok… I'll figure it out, while you get me out of here."

"Got it, I'll be checking in soon." He stood up to leave, and Dame stayed behind.

"What you got planned?" Dame asked once the door closed all the way.

"I don't know, but bro, I need you to take care of my wife and my seed."

"You gon' be out of here soon bro. I'm meeting up with Destini when I leave here so we can play clean up."

"No."

"What you mean no?" Dame's face was twisted up as he looked at me.

"Destini need to keep her hands clean, and you," I said, pointing my finger in his direction. "You need to sit the fuck down and make sure we still making money. We closed that chapter, and I'm not tryna go back, ya feel me?"

"I hear that— but ain't no way we getting outta here clean. Normal gon' be a problem."

"Imma handle that."

"How?"

I looked my brother in the eye as the CO knocked on the door to signal the end of the visit. "Don't worry about that; you just focus on doing what I said, and I got the rest."

"Aite, big bro. Keep yo head up in here. I know niggas ain't stupid, but just in case some niggas wanna make a name for themselves, ya know?"

"Heard you." He gave me a brotherly hug, and I was led down the hall to my private cell.

It was still a fuckin' cage at the end of the day, but I was comfortable. When I made it to my cell, I saw the phone Dame had one of the COs bring in for me, and I stuffed it in my pocket.

I laid down, and my mind drifted off to Karter. I couldn't wait to get my wife back in my arms again.

This shit was crazy! Just when I step away from the illegal shit and think I'm getting my life on the right path; then, I get jammed up and got bodies being pinned to me. I was gon' have a head full of gray hair before I even got to my 30th birthday. I was getting too old for this shit.

Chapter Three

Dame

"Yo?"

"Maaannn... bro tripping." I called Destini as I stomped out of the prison and to my car.

"What you mean?"

"It's a no go for us."

"Fuck that shit."

"That's what I said; his ass wanna act like he got all the answers, but he sitting in a fuckin' cage!" I punched the steering wheel and started my engine.

"Imma go pay a visit to the judge later on, this shit need to move a little faster than what it is."

"Nah, you need to chill." That was one thing I agreed with Dez on. I ain't like my lil' sis out here catching bodies, even if I was the one to teach her everything she knows.

"You over there turning pussy too? Maaaan, you niggas fall in love and get soft."

Click!

Destini hung up on my ass, and I had to shake my head at her. I was just as war ready as she was, but we had to move smart.

I drove the 30-minute ride back home, with a million thoughts running through my mind.

When I got home, Melodee's car was gone, so I called her and she answered on the first ring.

"Yessss, Damien Wright?" I heard a bunch of noise in the background, and it sounded like her ass was at a party or some shit.

"Ay, where the fuck you at?"

"Minding my business, why?"

"You love popping that hot shit, I got you when you get to the house."

"I'm just playing, Dame. Me and Karter went to do some shopping, I'll be back to the house soon. You need something?"

"Nah, I was just tryna see where you was at. How she holding up?"

"She good. Did you hear anything about Dez?" She was whispering, and I figured Karter must've been near her.

"Not really, I'll talk to you when you get home, though. Hurry up, I need a release."

"I'm on my way, daddy."

When she said that shit, I instantly bricked up.

Melodee got on my damn nerves sometimes, but I loved the shit outta her irritating ass. I took a shower and laid in the bed, smoking the pre-rolled L I had waiting.

***

"Mmmm, fuck!"

I thought I was dreaming I was getting some pussy, until I smelled that fruity shit Mel used in her hair. When I opened my eyes, she was looking down at me, biting her lips as she rode me like a pro. I flipped her over on her back, hooked her legs in my arms, and entered her roughly. Melodee was moaning and biting her lip, and her love faces were sexy as fuck.

"What's that shit you was talkin' earlier, Mel?" I pumped in and out of her vigorously and had to think about unicorns and granny panties so I wouldn't cum yet.

"I don't hear you Mel, huh?"

"Ahhh… nothiiiing! Shit!"

"Yeah, I thought so." I pulled out and flipped her over so she was on all fours. She started throwing her ass back on me, and I had a death grip on her waist. Man… my view right now was lovely as fuck. Melodee had one of them onion booties, and that shit was clapping with every stroke I delivered. I couldn't hold my nut anymore, and let my kids swim all inside of her.

"Uuuhh. Ggrrrrrr." I started growling like a damn grizzly bear; that's how good that shit felt to let go. Me and Mel hadn't fucked in a couple days because she been busy tryna cheer Karter up, and I been busy tryna get my damn brother outta jail. I couldn't believe they had my big bro in there like a fuckin' animal, man. I swear, I can't wait to kill some damn body.

"Bae, what's wrong?"

I looked down and realized I was still on top of her. I rolled off her and stood up so I could go piss.

"I know you heard me, Damien. What the hell is wrong with you?"

"Nothing." I tried to close the door so I could piss, and she kicked the shit back open.

"Don't be closing doors and shit, ain't no privacy in this bitch. If you want to close doors, you can be single."

"Mel... what the fuck are you talkin' about? I'm just tryna piss, and you kicking doors like you Bruce Lee or some shit."

"I like Jackie Chan— better." I stared at her as I peed, and she was dead ass serious right now, with her arms folded across her chest. I'm tellin' y'all, this girl was crazy as hell.

When I finished handling my business, I finally answered her. "I was thinkin' 'bout Dez. It's fuckin' with me 'cause I can't get my bro out that fuckin' cage."

I walked past her and sat on the bed. Melodee came in the room right behind me and climbed in my lap. She took my face in her small hands and looked me in the eyes.

"Bae, you can't go out here running on emotions. That'll be the time you fuck up and if you leave me, I will kill you."

"I ain't going nowhere no time soon, so just chill, Mel." I gave her a tap on her ass, telling her to get up, and she got up.

"I'm 'bout to go make me a sandwich, I'm hungry as hell. You want one?"

"Yeah, and I want some jalapenos on there instead of pickles."

"I got you, bae."

I grabbed my phone and went to the kitchen. I pulled everything I needed for our sandwiches out the fridge, and put it on the counter. Before I started on making them, I sent a text to our lawyer to see if he had any word yet.

Me: yo Ivan, I need an update

I tapped my finger as I watched the three dots signifying he was responding, and I was getting impatient.

Ivan: Wednesday he goes in front of the judge, be there at 9am

Me: who's the judge?

Ivan: Manley. Can you inform his wife? I left a message, but just in case she doesn't listen to it?

Me: Got you, thanks.

I put my phone up and made our sandwiches. When I came back in the room, Mel was on Facetime with Karter, so I laid next to her so I could get in the camera.

"Wassup, sis? How you holding up?"

"Hey Dame, I'm doing better. I'm waiting for on your brother to call me now, then I'll be great."

"I just spoke to his lawyer."

Her eyes got big and she was moving around, and I saw her sitting up in bed. "What did he say?"

"He goes in front of the judge in two days, so we gotta get bro a clean ass suit."

"Oh my God, thank you, I can't wait to finally see him. Do you want to go with me, or should I just take Mel?"

"Nah, y'all gon' ahead and do ya' lil girl thang. I trust yo taste, you know what bro like."

"Ok, I think this him Facetiming me, I gotta go."

She hung up and me and Mel sat in bed eating, then she turned on the TV, so I turned over to go to sleep. Even though I just woke up not too long ago, I was still tired as hell.

"Damn bae, you just woke up."

"I'm tired as fuck, bae. I been on E for a minute. You done took all my energy, so I need to replenish."

"Ok, goodnight."

"Goodnight, baby."

Chapter Four

Karter

I accepted the Facetime from the unknown number quickly, and when I saw my husband's smiling face, I was grinning like a fool.

"Hey, beautiful."

"Hey, handsome. How the hell do you got a cellphone, Dez?" I whispered into the camera.

"What are you whispering for, Karter?"

"I don't know, don't you got a cellmate or something?"

He laughed and shook his head. "Naw baby, I'm in this room by myself."

"Room?"

"Hell yeah, I need my damn privacy." The fact that he sitting here acting like he was on vacation on some shit had me shaking my head.

"Ok, anyway, I heard you see a judge Wednesday. Are you nervous?"

"Naw, I ain't got nothing to be nervous about." I'm glad he was so confident because I wasn't.

"Well, I can't wait to see you. I wish you would let me come up there and visit you."

"I don't want you in here, ma, This ain't no place you need to be. Plus, these niggas ain't 'bout to beating off to my wife. I'll kill one of they ass."

I laughed, but Dez held a serious expression on his face. "You crazy as hell, ain't nobody going to look at me. Anyway, I'm going to get your suit tomorrow. Is there a certain color you want to wear?"

"Nah, you pick whatever you want to, baby." He licked his lips in the camera, and I had to cross my legs before I got myself worked up for nothing.

"I can't wait until all of this is over and behind us."

"Soon—"

"I know, Dez; that's all you keep saying: *soon*. I'm tired of hearing that shit," I snapped.

"Imma blame that little spazzing moment on my baby fuckin' with yo head, so Imma let it go. You need to focus on getting back in the studio, BUT, take it easy. Have you looked at assistants yet?"

"No, but I—"

"Do it. I know it ain't gon' be tomorrow or no shit, but at least Thursday morning. No matter what, I want you to get up, get yo ass to the studio, and make sure them pigs cleaned they mess up before your first practice."

"And what if they didn't?"

"Then, I'll find somebody to come do the parking lot over, and maybe get you a new logo put on the window. We gon' have y'all lil' dancing asses all on the TV."

We laughed, and it felt good that at least he was in spirits. That's one thing I can say about Dez; he could have the weight of the world on his shoulders, but you wouldn't know it just by talking to him.

"You over there smiling, you not gon' say nothing?"

"I'm listening and mentally noting the things I have to do, bae."

"I ain't playing with you, girl."

"Okaaaaay, I promise, I'll handle my business Thursday morning."

"No matter what."

The way he said it… was like he knew we were going to hear something bad Wednesday. But, I kept my opinion to myself and said, "No matter what."

"Aite, now. I gotta be up early as hell, so Imma let you go. Feed my son again before you go to bed. I love you, Mrs. Wright."

"I love you too, Mr. Wright." I tried to hold a strong face, but my lip was quivering and a few tears fell before I wiped them away.

"Come on, Bugs; don't do this to me. You gotta be strong, mama. I love you, I gotta go."

He stayed in the camera for ten more seconds before he hung up. I laid in bed, and cried for about an hour before this fat baby had me getting up for snacks.

I ended up grabbing some orange sherbet and Chips Ahoy, and sat on the couch watching *Riverdale*. I didn't know why I was addicted to this show; it started off reminding me of *Pretty Little Liars*. If Dez was here, he would be huffing and puffing through the entire show. Wednesday couldn't come soon enough.

***

Walking into the courtroom, I felt a cold chill creep up my spine. I'd been in trouble before, but I swear I hated the inside of the courtroom.

Dame, Destini, Mel, and I all took the seats in the front that were directly behind where Dez would be sitting. When Dez came out wearing the all black Armani suit I picked for him, I was licking my lips extra hard. The officer let his hands free from the cuffs, and he held his arms out for me. I almost fell over the little divider when I made it to him.

"I guess you missed me, huh?"

"Yeah, I missed you stupid."

"Ok, Mr. Wright, you have to take your seat." His lawyer interrupted our moment, so I backed up and sat in my seat next to Melodee. The bailiff introduced the judge as he made his way up to his seat, and he had the ugliest scowl on his face.

My foot was tapping, and my hands were shaking as I listened to these people try to make my husband out to be some type of monster who just got around assaulting people. All of this for him knocking that one officer out? I wasn't stupid; I knew it had to be something else they were trying to get out of this case.

"Alright, I've heard enough to proceed from here, unless anyone has anything else to say?"

The prosecutor cleared his throat and stood up with a yellow folder in his hand. The bailiff took it and brought it to the judge, and Dez's lawyer looked as lost as we did.

"Your honor, as you can see, Mr. Wright is being investigated for a murder that took place outside of his wife's dance studio, as well as a murder of a young lady whom he had ties with. To ensure no other dead bodies pop up tied to Mr. Wright, he should be held without bail until this trial is over."

"WHAT?!?" I jumped out of my seat with steam coming out of my ears. There were a lot of murmurs in the courtroom as Melodee tried to pull me back down in my seat and keep Dame in his.

"Objection, your Honor! My client has not been charged with anything, and whatever case he's mentioning has nothing to do with the current case at hand!" Dez's lawyer was up out of his seat, and his white face was a bright shade of red.

Dez looked back at me, and it felt like the walls were closing in on me.

I should just confess so they won't hold him. I can't let him sit in jail for something I did.

The loud banging of the judge's gavel snapped me out of my thoughts.

"Order! Order! I need everyone to get themselves together. Now, I'm going to ignore the last couple minutes of outbursts and get right to business." He wiped the sweat off his forehead, and handed the folder in his hand back to the bailiff. "Mr. Montgomery, you know that is not how things are handled in my courtroom. Let that be the last time.

Now… Mr. Wright, these are some pretty serious charges that are in front of you. Officer Sanchez suffered from a broken jaw and nose from the hit you gave him. This is a felony, and something I can't let slide. But, I'm feeling generous and since you don't have any priors, I took that into consideration. You're ordered to serve a total of 60 days in the Cook County Correctional Facility, and to pay a fine of $250,000. Considering the circumstances, Mr. Wright, consider yourself lucky." The judge hit his gavel and stood up to leave.

"Karter, come here," Dez called out to me, and I lifted my head out of my lap to look at him. He wiped my tears and gave me a long kiss on the lips. "Don't cry, remember what you promised me. I'll call you when I can, ok?"

He was pulled away, and I walked out the courtroom to meet up with everybody else. Dame and Destini stormed out after the judge spoke, and Melodee was keeping them calm. The ride back home was quiet as everyone was stuck in their thoughts. Sixty days wasn't a lot of time, but it was when I had to think of the time I had to spend away from Dez.

Dame pulled up in front of our home, and I didn't want to go in. "I'll come spend a night with you, bestie. We gon' get through this," Melodee said as she looked back at me.

I gave everyone a forced smile and got out the car. Dame sat in the driveway until I went all the way inside the house. When the front door closed behind me, I leaned on it and slid down to the floor.

I knew I told Dez that I was going to be strong, but first I needed to get all my tears out.

I couldn't wait to cuss his ass out later.

Chapter Five

Dezmund 'Dez'

"I promise, I'm working to get you out of here soon, just be patient with me." Ivan was sweating and flipping through the folder he got from the sneaky ass prosecutor.

"It's not like I got a choice but to be patient. What does that say, though?" I pointed to the file in his hand, and he straightened up his posture.

"There's nothing that ties you to this, other than it being outside of your wife's business. Did you have something to do with this?"

"I didn't do it," was all I said to answer his question. Ivan had been around for a while, but I didn't know what type of listening devices or shit they had in here, so I was keeping it short.

He nodded his head, and something behind me caught his attention. I turned around to see a detective walking into the private room we were in.

"Sorry to interrupt, but I figured I'd save us some time and meet you here. I'm Detective Normal, and I'm working the murder of Kevin Martin. I had a few questions for your client." The detective helped herself to a seat and pulled it up next to me.

Ivan straightened his tie and closed the folder he had in front of him. "I don't see how my client could be of any assistance in your case, Detective."

"Mr. Wright knows how he can be of assistance to me. My victim is actually his wife's father." I sat unbothered by the whole act she was putting on as she waited for me to respond.

"Do you know this person she's speaking of?" Ivan looked over at me, and I simply shook my head and folded my hands in my lap.

"Can't say I know anyone by that name."

"Well, maybe I should pay Mrs. Wright a visit. It seems like murder is following her; maybe I'm sniffing up the wrong tree." My jaw clenched when she mentioned my wife, and I wanted to smack the smug look off this bitch's face.

"Ahem." Ivan cleared his throat to stop me from speaking, and I was biting my lip so hard I started to taste blood. "If you don't mind, my client and I would like to finish going over our case alone."

"No problem, I'll be in touch. Don't go anywhere, Dezmund." The way she said my name had my skin crawling. I knew she was going to be a problem.

"You know where the find me for the next 60 days."

***

The next day after I saw the judge, I officially started my countdown. Fifty-nine more days until I was out this bitch. After I got off the phone with Karter last night, I knew I had to think of a plan fast before her crazy ass went to confess to murder.

"Wassup bro, how you holding up?" I called Destini, and she answered on the first ring.

"Tomorrow, ride with Dame here; we got some unfinished business to address."

"I got you. How you holding up in there, big homie? You ain't made no new friends in there, have you?"

"Keep playing if you want. I'm only gon' be in this bitch for two months."

"Damn, man… I can't believe they on that with you."

"Don't start, I'll see you tomorrow. Take care of my mama."

I walked out my "cell" to go sit outside and think, and these niggas was watching my every move. Of course, mothafuckas knew who I was. The Wright last name held weight itself. On the yard, I sat far away from everyone where I had a perfect view of everything, and everyone.

I sat here thinking… and I knew the only way this shit with Karter's pops was going to go away was if Detective Normal was gone. I really wasn't tryna kill no damn cop. I was never gon' see my seed grow.

Somebody approaching me caught my attention, so I stood up. He walked up to me nervous as hell, and I had to size him up. He looked like he was a few years younger than me, but if he came over here on some bullshit, I was gon' beat his little ass out here.

When he got within arm's reach, I held my hand up, signaling him to stay right there, then I put my hands in my pocket. He threw his hands up to show he didn't have anything, then put his arms by his side.

"I didn't come over here on nothing like that, I see how you lookin' at me. I-I was just trying to see if you had some work on the outside, a job opening maybe?"

"What kinda work you tryna do? I got a club and daycare. You good with kids?"

"Not THAT kind of work. You know, your *other* line of business." I squinted my eyes at him and looked around the yard.

"You got the wrong person, bro, sorry." I sat back down, and he just stood there. "You rethinking that position?"

"Come on, man. I know exactly who you are. I'm just trying to get on so I can get my daughter back. I ain't even tryna be doing it for long."

"What's your name, man?"

"Kolby— JaKolby Davis."

"What you in here for?" He shook his head and looked at the ground. "How you tryna get into some big boy work and can't even look me in my eyes when I'm talking to you? That ain't even a nigga I can trust."

"I stole some diapers and shit for my daughter from Walgreens. Like I told you, I need money. They got my little girl in one of these damn homes until I can prove I got money to take care of her."

"You know how to count?"

"Yeah, I ain't no dummy."

"Aite, lil nigga. Don't let that mouth get you in trouble. I might have something for you, I'll find you tomorrow."

"Thanks, man." He turned around and ran back to the basketball court, and I stood up so I could go back inside.

"Hold on, Wright, you can't go inside just yet."

"Why the fuck not?"

"Random search, and they got word to move you to B block."

"Word from who?" I was pissed hearing this shit; somebody was testing the fuck outta me.

"I don't know, boss."

I ran my hand down my face and walked away. I texted my lawyer and Dame to get up here ASAP, and put my phone back up.

After sitting outside for another twenty minutes, the CO waved me over to come inside, and I walked behind him to my new cell, I guess. This little ass, six by eight cage was gon' drive me fuckin' crazy. That wasn't even the worse part— these mothafuckas thought I was about to be in this bitch with another nigga? Naahhh, they had me fucked up.

"Ay, CO! Tell the Warden I need to be seeing him soon." He nodded and walked off.

I see I was gon' have to temporarily come outta retirement.

Chapter Six

Destini

"Tell my baby I said I love him when you get there, Dest, I'm not playing."

"Okaaaayy Ma, I'll call you later." I hung up the phone and sat back in my seat.

"What you been doing, sis? You looking stressed."

"Shit, I am. I'm tired of seeing this damn prison, man. Then, I'm tryna figure out what the hell to do with myself. It's boring as fuck sitting in the house."

"Maaaan, figure something out. Open up a fuckin' ice cream parlor or some shit."

Dame found a parking spot outside of the jail, and we got out the car. I wasn't even gon' respond to the dumb shit he said because we were gon' end up fighting out here.

Ivan was waiting in the lobby for us, and after we were searched, they led us to a private room. Dez came in a few minutes later, and he was looking pissed.

"Ivan, find out who put word in to have me moved to a fucking cage, and get that shit fixed. And see what you can do for a kid named JaKolby. Get back to me right away with that. You can go."

Ivan scurried out the room like it was on fire, and I turned my full attention back to Dez. "What's going on, bro?"

"Detective Normal is a pain in my ass. Bitch showed up after court, talkin' about that shit that happened this weekend. She's trying to bring Karter in it, and my baby can't go through that."

"What you want us to do?" Dame asked, sitting up with his hands folded on the table.

"Nothing yet, until I get out of here. Have somebody keep an eye on her and see who she talking to and what she knows."

"And, who is this JaKolby kid?" I asked the question I had been dying to know since he said the name.

"Somebody that needs help, and Imma help him. WE gon' help him. You figure out what you gon' do about money now?"

"Not yet."

"Dest—"

"Dez, come on, I got it. Chill." The rest of our unplanned visit went smooth as we caught up on the last few days.

Dame dropped me off at home, and I stayed up all night trying to think about my next career choice. I had never been the nine to five type, and I didn't know shit about how a business worked… but I was gon' make it happen.

***

Two Weeks later…

"I like this spot, I'll take it." I decided that I was gon' open up a clothing and sneaker store, and I found the perfect location on 95th and Western.

"Great, I can get your papers drawn up, and I'll be right back with you." I watched the thick realtor sashay her way out the door, and her ass was fat as hell.

I did another walk-through of the spot, and I was glad this was a new spot so nothing big needed to be done to the inside. Once the realtor came back with all the papers I needed to sign, I wrote her a check and got the keys to *Wright Trends*.

When I locked up and left, I was feeling accomplished as fuck. When I was riding around, Dez called me so, I connected it through the car's Bluetooth.

"Wassup?"

"I need you to drop a care package off at this address I'm about to send you."

"Got you, bro."

"What you up to?"

"Shiiiittt, ya girl just got the keys to my new establishment. Wright Trends about to blow up, big homie."

"Good shit, I'm proud of you, but don't forget what I told you to do."

"I got you."

"Destini, go check on Karter for me. Make sure she ain't stressing." I agreed, and we got off the phone.

I called Karter and headed home so I could take care of what Dez asked me to.

"Wassup, Destini?"

"Shit, just checking on you, making sure you ain't over there drinking and shit. I don't need my lil' niece or nephew to come out with 13 fingers and shit."

"Shut up, fool. I'm good, at the studio now checking on stuff."

"Aaaaand, I need you and Mel's help with something."

"I knew it was something else. Black people can't never call and say hi. What you need help with though, boo?"

"I'm tryna get this sneaker store up and running, and I need yo help."

"Awww, that's good. Whatever you need help with, just let me know and I'll come through."

"Good looking. You gone head and handle yo shit over there, and I'll holla at you." I pulled up to my home in Calumet City and got out the car.

Whenever Dez said he wanted to drop a care package off to somebody, he was talking about cash. Dez was always giving back to the those who needed help, and I admired that about my big brother. Even though he was as savage as they came, he had a big heart. I grabbed a brown envelope and stuffed a couple stacks of wrapped hundreds in it. The address he sent me was in Calumet Park, which was about 15 minutes away from me. I drove the short distance and was parked in front of a small ranch style house. I got out the car and went to knock on the front door.

A short, sexy dark-skinned girl opened the door, and I was licking my lips as I got a good look at her. She had her hair up in a bun, and she had on some paint splattered overalls, and a sports bra underneath. Her left arm was covered in tatts of flowers and shit, but I was diggin' it.

"Can I help you?" Her soft voice snapped me out my thoughts, and I forgot why I was here for a minute.

"Naw, but I could definitely help you. What's your name, sweetheart?"

"It's Jakira, but really… what can I do for you?" She peeked her head outside and looked up and down the street. Shit, I did the same thing; she was acting like somebody was coming for her ass.

"My bad, baby girl... here you go. Take care of yourself."

I handed her the envelope and turned to walk back to my car. I noticed Jakira still standing in the doorway, so I gave her a smile before I pulled off. Shiiiitt, I need something new anyway. Tiffany's ass been getting on my nerves lately, always asking for money and shit instead of getting a damn job.

I knew one thing, though: Ms. Jakira was gon' be seeing me again.

Chapter Seven

Karter

"Ok ladies, this was good. I'm so proud of y'all! Tomorrow, I'm not going to be here, but there will still be practice. Tori knows what to do, and y'all better do what she said or you gon' have to deal with me. There's a Thanksgiving competition. Anybody that is late or doesn't show up will NOT participate. Got it?"

"Yessss." I looked around at each Diva, then dismissed them when I was sure they understood that I was serious.

Once all the girls were gone, I grabbed my bag and shut all the lights out. Tori waited for me to leave, and we walked out together. When I posted that I was looking for an assistant, Tori were one of the best dancers who came to try out. You damn right I had tryouts for an assistant. You can't *assist* me with shit if you can't dance.

"Drive safe, Tori. Call me if you need anything tomorrow."

"Thanks. You too, Kay." We got in our cars and pulled away in opposite directions.

I stopped at Portillo's to grab something to eat before I went home, because I was craving an Italian beef.

There was an unmarked car sitting in front of the gate, and I got nervous as I approached it. Detective Normal got out of the car when I pulled up next to her, and I rolled my eyes before I let the window down.

"How are you doing this evening, Mrs. Wright?"

"I'm fine, how can I help you?"

"Do you have time to come down and answer a few questions?"

"Now?"

"Yes, we can do this inside, or you could meet me at the precinct."

"I'll meet you at the precinct," I answered and rolled my window back up. This was not something I wanted to deal with right now, or ever for that matter.

I waited until the detective pulled off before I opened the gate. I was about to eat my food before I did anything. Whatever the hell she wanted could wait.

While I ate my food, I called Dez and prayed he answered. "What's up, bae? I only got a few minutes, before these bitches make rounds."

"The detective was waiting outside of the house when I got here. She wants me to come down to answer questions. What am I supposed to do?"

"Just be cool, baby. Go down there; whatever she asks, you don't have to answer, I'll have Ivan waiting for you there, ok?"

"Ok."

"How my baby doing? When do you go back to the doctor?"

"I go tomorrow, and in two more weeks, I'll officially be out of the first trimester, bae. I'm so excited. I wish you could be here to go with me." It had been a few weeks since he got his sentence, and I swear, every day that was supposed to be better felt worse.

"You already know how I feel about that. I been counting down the days until I can be inside my wife again. Imma call you at our regular time tonight, baby. I gotta go, love you."

I rolled my eyes at his inappropriate comment and hung up the phone. I decided to call Melodee because if I had to go up here, she was coming with me.

"Hey chica, what you up to?"

"Can you come somewhere with me? Like now?" I had to be specific with Melodee; her ass would have me waiting until next week or some shit.

"Yeah, I guess so. I wasn't doing shit anyway. Here I come."

I waited for Mel outside, and hopped in her car when she arrived. When I told her where I had to go and why, she drove us to the precinct and was cursing the whole time there.

"I know they not gon' let me in here, so I'll be waiting in the lobby. If you need backup, just yell hooty hoo or something."

"Backup for what, Mel? I swear, you be around Dame too much." I walked to the front desk and let them know who I was there for.

Seconds later, Detective Normal came from the back and ushered me to a room. It was identical to the room I was held in before, and my stomach started doing flips.

"Have a seat, Mrs. Wright. Thank you for coming."

"Not that I had a choice, with you popping up at my home and all."

"Well, we take murder very seriously here."

"Who was killed?" I asked with my eyebrows bunched.

"I find it funny that you don't know anything about your father being killed outside of your place of business. Was it open that night?"

"What night was that?"

She slammed the file she was holding on the table and opened it up. She showed me pictures of Kevin and Jazz's bodies, and I pushed them away from me.

"Don't tell me you never saw a dead body before, Mrs. Wright?"

Before I could answer, Ivan came busting in the room, and Mel was right behind him. "This little fishing expedition you're on is over. You will not keep harassing my clients. Let's go, Mrs. Wright. Sorry it took so long."

"It's fine, Ivan. Not speaking with you, Detective Normal." I followed Ivan out of the door, and he stopped me in the parking lot when we made it to the car.

"What did you say? If she asked you anything about Dezmund, it can't be used in court."

"Ivan, relax. I didn't say anything. She had just shoved pictures of dead bodies in my face before you came in."

"Ok, I'm going to file a harassment suit against her. At least then, it'll give us some time to figure this out."

"Thanks, Ivan. Have a good evening."

Melodee and I got in the car, and she drove off toward my house.

"Kay, you still haven't told me what happened that night."

Just thinking about it put a dark cloud over my mood. I was debating if I wanted to tell her or not. I trusted Mel with my life, and I knew she'd never do anything to snake me, but I didn't wanna put this burden on her.

"I'm waiting, Karter."

"Wait until we get inside, I promise I'll tell you."

The rest of the ride was quiet, besides the sound of the radio. I didn't know what was on Melodee's mind, but I was trying to figure out what I should do. Dez said he was taking care of things, but I needed to do something to help.

Mel walked in the house and didn't give me a chance to get comfortable before she was asking questions. "Ok, so what the hell happened? Cuz you niggas being real top secret. First, you're being blamed for Jazz's murder, now your father—"

"That's not my father."

"He nutted in yo mama, and you were born months later… that's ya damn pappy, whether you want it to be or not. That's not my concern, though. I know you're holding something from me, Karter. Come on, we're best friends. Been best friends since foreveeerrr."

"Okaaaayy, damn… you irritating as hell. Well, for starters, I didn't kill Jazz. I didn't even know the broad was dead. But… I did kill Kevin."

Melodee gasped loudly, and her eyes bucked. Her mouth was opening and closing, like she was trying to find her words and couldn't.

"He had a gun to Dez, and I thought he was going to kill him. I didn't know what else to do. My mom popped up, talking about he wanted to rob us, and I don't even know how he knew where my studio was. It happened so fast, I didn't even look." I was crying so hard my body was shaking, and Melodee just wrapped her arms around me, hugging me tightly. This was going to hunt me for the rest of my life, but if I had to do it all over again, I wouldn't hesitate to protect my husband.

***

Bzzzz.... Bzzzz

The loud sound of my phone vibrating on the table had me jumping out of my sleep, and I was looking around confused. I didn't remember falling asleep, but Mel was petty for leaving me on the couch.

My phone went off again, and I saw it was a FaceTime from Dez. "Hey baby. Sorry, I was asleep."

"Maaannn, you can't be doing that to me. You ok?"

"Yeah, I'm fine. The detective is going to a thorn in our ass, bae. She—"

"Don't worry about all that, I keep telling you I got it."

Instead of going back and forth with him about it, I just didn't say nothing. I checked to make sure the door was locked, then went to the kitchen.

"You got an attitude now, Karter?"

"NoPe, I'm good." I made sure to add extra emphasis on the P.

"So why you— man, I'll call you in the morning." Dez hung up, and I was stuck looking like at the phone like he was still going to be on it.

I couldn't believe he fucking hung up on me, all because I said I *didn't* have an attitude.

Crazy ass Gemini shit.

It was too late for me to cook anything, so I just grabbed what I needed for a sandwich and sat at the island.

Bing!

My text notification went off, and I picked it up to see a message from Dez.

Dez: *I'm sorry bae, this shit stressful as fuck, and I can't be worried about you out here tryna play Bonnie and shit. I don't need that, I just need my wife to handle business. I love you, and I'll Facetime you at the regular time in the morning. Forever.*

I smiled at the message before I replied. My baby was bipolar as hell in there. I couldn't wait until he came home. After I ate my sandwich, I went to bed to prepare for my big day tomorrow. I had my first scheduled ultrasound, and I couldn't wait to have those pictures to show his crazy daddy.

***

"What the hell?" I was driving to my doctor's appointment when I noticed a white Chevy Malibu with Indiana plates following me.

When I pulled into the parking lot of the office, the car was still behind me. I grabbed my purse and made sure my mace was in my hand before I got out.

The driver was a short, dark-skinned girl who I'd never seen before, and she was stomping up to me.

"Are you Karter?" She was mugging me, and I was mugging her ass right back. I didn't know what the hell this chick's problem was, but she needed to go on and find her some business before I was late.

"And, who are you?"

"Chloe... I know what you did to Jazz. She was my best friend, and I'm going to make sure you pay for what you did!" She turned and got back in her car, and I went inside for my appointment. This was too much going on at one time.

Once I was checked in at the front desk, I sat down and texted Melodee.

Me: I need to go on vacation, I'm going to lose my fucking mind, Mel!

Melodee: What happened?

Me: Apparently, Jazz's friend is in town to prove that I killed her. Why is all this BS happening to me?!

"Karter Wright?"

I put my phone up and followed the nurse to the back. She took my weight, blood pressure, and gave me a cup to pee in.

"When you're done, just stick it in the little window, stay undressed from the waist down, and we'll be right with you."

Once I was done in the bathroom, I put the cup where she told me and went back to the room. The doctor came in a moment later. For five minutes, she stood here telling me what I should expect and all this other stuff, when all I cared about was this ultrasound.

"Alright, gone ahead and lay back for me, and open your legs wide."

She turned the light low, and I laid back on the bed. When she put that damn probe inside of me, I wanted to kick her in the head. It's not like it was hurting; it was just uncomfortable as hell. After she took all the pictures she needed, she turned the camera toward me, and I got a look at my little peanut.

"That flickering right there is the heartbeat." She turned the volume up, and I heard my baby's heartbeat echoing through the room.

"Everything looks good. Make an appointment to get some bloodwork done, and I'll see you in about three to four weeks."

"Thank you." She walked out, and I got myself cleaned up before I put my clothes back on. I grabbed the pictures she left on the table and made my next appointment.

When I was walking to my car, Destini called me, and she was smacking in my ear.

"What you doing, sis?"

"What are you eating that damn loud?" I got in the car and let my phone connect to the Bluetooth.

"My bad, I had some Now and Laters. You know them bitches be gettin' stuff in yo teeth and shit. But ay, can you meet me somewhere?"

"Where? I don't feel like driving all over the world."

"I'm right here on Western, bring yo lazy ass on."

I rolled my eyes and went to the address Destini sent me. It was a store in a strip mall, and it had *Wright Trends* on the front. I swear, this damn family didn't know how to sit down. Melodee's car pulled beside me, and she had the same crazy look I had.

Chapter Eight

Melodee

What in the hell did this girl do now?

I got out my car and met Karter on the sidewalk. "What the hell is this?"

"I don't know; she called and asked me to meet her here."

"Hey y'all, come in. Why the hell you standing outside looking crazy for anyway?"

We followed her into the building, and it was empty as hell. There was maroon paint on the wall, and a black counter sitting on the other side of the room.

"And what's this supposed to be?" I asked, looking around again.

"A clothing store... but, I need y'alls help. I don't want just my style in here. I need that girly shit y'all wear too."

"Ohhhh, let me see what I can do in here." I was rubbing my hands like Birdman as I pictured everything I could put in here.

"Nah, I just need yo' help with yo' clothes. I got everything else."

"Girl, you better ask yo' brothers how I handle business, stop playing."

We discussed the store for a while, until Karter got to talking about how she was hungry. Our little meeting ended up at Potbelly's, and I was banging my sandwich as Karter talked to Destini about getting a small section for kid clothes.

"I ain't putting no kids' clothes in there. I ain't tryna have all them damn bebe's kids running through my shit." Her phone rang, and her face balled up before she stuck it back in her pocket. "I gotta go, but I'll holla at y'all later." Destini slid out the booth, leaving me and Karter to talk.

"So, are you gon' tell Dez about ol' girl's friend being here?"

Karter shook her head and put her shake down. "I don't know, I don't need him flipping out over nothing. But then again, I ain't tryna hear his mouth if he finds out another way. Huuuhh!" She rolled her eyes up to the ceiling and sat back in her seat.

"You should've got her number so we could've linked. You can't do nothing, but I'll gladly drag that bitch around the world."

Karter laughed as she finished up her sandwich and looked at her phone. "Hubby gon' be calling soon, so I gotta go."

"You ain't shit." We walked together across the street to our cars and pulled off at the same time.

My next stop was to check on the club because there was going to be a party there tomorrow for some basketball player. I didn't follow sports, and I wasn't gon' pretend like I did. What I was going to follow was that check, and I was gon' throw this man the best damn birthday party of his life.

****

I got to the house and, as always, Dame's ass wasn't there. Ever since Dez got sentenced, his ass had been ghost in here. I mean, I understood he trying to help his brother and Karter, but damn— what about your girl?

Me: Are you going to be out late again?

I sat looking at my phone for five minutes, and I got no response. "Ok, this nigga got until I get out the shower, or I'm going off," I spoke aloud as I went in the bathroom, and wrapped my hair up.

I got in the shower and made sure to take my time to let the hot water beat down on my back. When I was done, I moisturized my body and finally checked my phone.

Nothing.

I called his phone and at first, it went straight to voicemail, so I called back and this time, it rang.

"Wassup?" he finally answered, and I heard the radio in the background.

"Why the fuck you ain't text me back? Where you at?"

"I ain't get no text from you, Mel, chill."

"Who the fuck got the text then, Dame? Because I texted and called you. I'm tired of this shit."

"What shit— man, I'll be home in like an hour, I'm tryna handle something."

"Well, I won't be here when you return, so bye." I hung up on him and laid back on the bed. I only said that to piss him off. I wasn't going nowhere, especially right now.

"Yo, Mel!"

I dozed off and woke up to Dame screaming my name. I was still only wearing my robe, so I closed it and sat Indian style in the middle of the bed.

"Fuck you gotta say all that stupid shit for? Got me speeding and shit. And you just gon' fuckin' sit there and smile?"

The look Dame was giving me was supposed to scare me, I guess, but it wasn't doing nothing but make me horny, and my southern lips were purring.

"You so sexy, bae." I reached for him, and he smacked my hands away.

"Naw, you said you was leaving, remember? Don't be tryna touch on me now."

"Ok, you want me gone? Bye, fuck." I jumped off the bed and shoulder-checked him as I walked by to get to my closet. He grabbed my robe and it fell to the floor, but I kept walking my naked ass to the closet to grab some clothes.

"Fuck you doing? Stop playing with me, man." Dame stood at the door and watched me move around my walk-in closet looking for something to wear.

"I ain't playing, move. I'm leaving."

He let me walk past him, then tackled me on the damn bed. When I tried to get up, his pushed my face into the bed forcibly, and I heard his belt buckle coming off. It took him long enough, shit. I knew what I needed; I was just waiting on him to figure it out.

Dame entered me roughly, and I was stuck moaning into the pillow.

"Damn, that shit wet as fuck. This all you wanted, Mel, huh?"

He leaned down and was planting kisses on my neck, never missing a beat with his strokes. My body was shaking as I came hard, and my body felt like it was about to give up on me. Dame pulled out of me and flipped me over onto my back. He was on his knees with his face buried in my honey pot, and I was trying to climb the bed to get away from him, but he had my legs locked in his arm.

He was smacking like he had a slab of ribs in front of him, and the feel of his beard on my already sensitive clit was driving me crazy.

"Let me taste that shit, Mel." His deep voice sent vibrations through my body, and I gave in and was cumming again. Dame stood up with my juices dripping from his beard and kissed me. I got into it and was sucking on his tongue.

"Yo freaky ass. Shit taste good, don't it? Get up and ride this dick, Mel."

I jumped up with the quickness and pushed Dame onto the bed. His shoes were still on with his pants around his ankles, so I helped him take them all the way off before I climbed on top of him. I eased down on him and was moving up and down slowly as I got adjusted to his size. No matter how much we did it, it still felt like the first time we had sex. We went at it for hours, until he finally got his second nut and I was beat.

He pulled me on his chest and kissed the top of my head. This was probably the most time we spent together in the last two or three weeks, and I was trying to enjoy every minute.

"I'm sorry, baby. I know I need to do better with this relationship shit. You wanna go out this weekend? I'll plan some stuff for us."

"That sounds good. Whatever you plan is fine."

I laid on Dame's, chest listening to the sound of his heartbeat until I finally fell asleep. I wouldn't replace this feeling for nothing in the world.

Chapter Nine

Dame

After Melodee fell asleep, I slid out the bed and went to take a quick shower. I still had shit to take care of. I just came home to make sure my girl ain't leave my ass. I wasn't gon' flex— I was scared as hell when she said that dumb shit, but I got why she was mad. All my time had been spent tryna get my brother out of jail and keep my sister in law out of jail. Clearing their names was number one. I'd be damned if my brother spent any more time behind bars.

"Yo?" I was getting dressed when I got a call from the lil' nigga I had watching Detective Normal.

"This pig bitch really determined to get some shit. She been stopping niggas in the hood, asking questions. You sure you don't want me to just handle this shit right now?"

I walked out the room and made sure Mel was still asleep before I answered. "Naw, just keep doing what you doing, and if it look like she spending too much time with one nigga… you know what to do."

"Aite, bro." I hung up and grabbed the keys to my car so I could leave. I set up a meeting on the other side of town with a pig we still had on our payroll. I needed some answers, and whatever evidence they had needed to disappear ASAP.

I left the house and hopped in my car, pulling out instantly. I needed this shit over— quick.

I walked into the bar and nodded to the owner before I walked to his back office. Detective Morris was already in the back, and he stood up to shake my hand when I entered.

"Fuck you want me to do with that?" I looked down at his hand like it was covered in baby shit and backed up.

"My bad." He put his hand down and sat back in his seat. I sat across from him and folded my hands on the table.

"What did you find out?"

"Well, for starters, Normal got it bad for y'all. I don't know what her problem is, but she's trying everything she can to have enough to charge y'all. Well, more so your brother."

"Ok, you need to get rid of whatever you can. I don't care how you do it, but make it happen."

"It's not that easy, she—"

"I don't give a fuck! Make the shit disappear, or that's yo' fuckin' ass!" I banged my fist on the table, and all the color drained from his face. Detective Morris was a skinny ass white dude that look like he should've been a science teacher instead of a fuckin' detective. He'd been working for us since he first joined the force. Nigga ain't give a damn about the oath he took. Money talked all day long.

"I… I got it. Is there anything else you need?"

"Naw, you can go." With that, he shot up out of his seat and left, leaving me to my thoughts.

I wasn't too much worried about nothing coming back to him with that Jaz shit, 'cause he wasn't even in the state. But, I knew if it came down to it, he was gon' take that murder charge so Karter wouldn't have to.

Mel: where the hell did you go?

"Shit." I got up and left out so I could go home. I knew she was about to be looking at me sideways for leaving in the middle of the night. I texted and told her I was on my way back and she didn't reply, but I saw she read it. That meant she was gon' be on some bullshit when I got back. It took me damn near forty-five minutes to make it home. When I pulled up, I saw Rock, my dog, sitting outside in his cage next to a pile of my shoes. I hopped out the car and ran in the house. I heard Melodee stomping around upstairs, so I went up the stairs three at a time to make it to her.

"Yo, what the fuck is yo' problem? Why the fuck my son outside?" She didn't even bother to look at me as she was throwing shit everywhere.

"You would rather be in the damn streets than at home with your girl, so you and that mutt can get the hell out."

"Nigga... you know this MY damn house, right?" She whipped her head around so fast, and her face had a nasty scowl on it. She stomped toward me and had her long ass nails pointing in my face.

"Aaawww, so now this YO' shit, right?"

I mean, if she was being technical, it was my damn house. I bought this shit, and she just moved in with me.

But, I ain't want to make this shit worse than it already was, so I just said, "You know that's not what I meant, bae. This is our house, so I don't understand why you packing my shit."

"We just had a whole conversation about this shit. So, you just said what you *thought* I wanted to hear so I could shut the fuck up, right?"

I ran my hands down my waves and blew out a deep breath. "I hate when you do that. Stop putting words in my mouth, Mel. I already had this meeting set up, so I had to go."

"Why not just tell me instead of tiptoeing out the damn house after I fall asleep?"

"I ain't tiptoe no fuckin' where, I'm a grown ass man."

She looked at me like she was offended, then nodded her head up and down. "Ok Damien, remember that." She pushed the suitcase she was packing onto the floor, then laid in the bed.

"Don't do no stupid shit, Mel. I ain't playing with yo' ass. You gon' make me choke the snot out yo' ass."

"Mmmhhmm, go get yo' ugly ass dog before he get sick." Melodee waved me off and started going through her phone.

Instead of continuing to go back and forth with her, I went to get Rock and put him in his house. He was looking up at me like his feelings were hurt, and I wanted to go drag Mel's ass out here to apologize to him.

"You good, man; her ass just tripping right now." It sounded like this nigga scoffed at me before he walked away. These damn pets were disrespectful as fuck nowadays, man.

When I made it back to the front door, it was closed, and I knew this petty ass girl locked the door on my ass. I rattled the knob and shook my head as I got my keys out my pocket. She had the damn alarm on and everything.

I walked upstairs to the room and saw she had this door locked too. I was gon' let her have this night, but tomorrow, I was nippin' all this shit, fa real.

When I woke up the next morning, Melodee was sitting at the table eating a bowl a cereal. "You good now?"

"I'm always good, Damien. I don't know what you talkin' about."

"We not doing this, Mel. I'm dealin' with enough shit, I need you to just work with me."

"I been working with you, Damien. When you gon' put some work in with me?!" My phone rang, interrupting me before I could respond, and I saw it was Dez.

"Go ahead and answer, Damien."

I sighed before I answered. "Wassup, bro?"

"Some bitch been following Karter around. Apparently, she somebody to Jazz. Send her ass back home—alive, Dame."

"I'll get somebody on it."

We hung up the phone, and I ran my hands down my beard. Grabbing my burner phone, I sent a text out to get that situation looked into before I turned my attention back to Melodee.

She was scrolling on her phone and still eating her cereal, so I sat next to her. "I promise you, once I get this squared away, Imma get us back on track."

"It's fine, take care of your family."

"You my family too, Melodee, damn. Stop with that stubborn bullshit."

87

"I'm good, I'm about to go check on my best friend." She stood up, put her bowl in the sink, and walked in the living room. A few minutes later, I heard the front door close and Melodee's car pulling out the driveway. I needed this shit handled ASAP before I fucked around and lost my mind, and my girl.

Chapter Ten

Destini

"I haven't seen or heard from you in almost two weeks, Dest! I call and text, and you don't answer. What the hell is going on?" I was at my store, watching the team I hired set up clothing racks, and I finally decided to answer the phone for her buggin' ass. I didn't tell Tiffany what I was doing 'cause I was lowkey tired of her ass. It was probably 'cause I had Jakira's fine ass on my mind. "Hello?! I know you hear me talkin' to you!"

"G! I'm fuckin' busy, and you need to chill the fuck out with all that yellin' and shit!" She had me fucked up, and I had to go to the back room to cuss her ass out.

"Either fix it, or I'm done." I looked at the phone and had to laugh.

"Bye." I hung up and walked back to the front of the store. I don't do ultimatums, so if she wanted to go, then two fingers.

After all the shelves and racks were set up. I paid my workers for the day and sent them home. All my merchandise was due to arrive tomorrow, and I couldn't wait to see all this shit put together. I let Melodee take over the clothing part, and I handled getting all the sneakers. Karter was too busy trying to keep herself above water, so I told her she didn't have to do anything. Dez still had fifteen days until he was released, and everybody had been on pins and needles with that detective bitch sniffing around. I didn't see why they wouldn't just let me off her ass and call it a day.

It was nine at night when I left the store, so I just took my ass home to order me some food and smoke until I passed out. I was tired as fuck from trying to make sure all this shit went as smoothly and quickly as possible.

"Yo?" Dez called when I was walking into the crib, so I had him on speaker while I rolled my L.

"I need you come scoop my homie, Kolby, up tomorrow by ten. He gon' start working with you too. I heard shit looking nice over there. I'm proud of you, man."

"It ain't shit, you know anything I touch is a hit."

"Fuck outta here, but don't forget, tomorrow by ten."

"Aite bro, I'll holla at you." This nigga was getting on my nerves running all these damn errands and shit. I knew they had muhfuckas that was willing to be they fuckin' gopher… and it sure as hell wasn't me.

***

Sitting outside of County, I was itching like a mothafucka to pull off. Finally, after I'd been sitting outside for twenty minutes, this nigga, Kolby, came walking to the car. I only knew it was him because Dez sent me his picture this morning. At first, I was pissed about getting up, but then I remembered his fine ass sister and perked up real quick.

"Wassup, I'm Kolby." He held his hand for me to shake it, so I did before I pulled off.

"Destini. I'll take you to the crib to get changed, but yo' ass gon' have thirty minutes to take the best shower of yo' life and get dressed, 'cause I got some shipments coming."

"Shipments? Maaann, Dez said I was gon' be legal now. I can't go back in that bitch."

"Nigga… I'm talking about clothes. I was thinking about making yo' simple ass my assistant manager, but

91

now it's a little iffy." We both started laughing, and I drove toward his house.

"My bad, I wasn't thinking straight. But that's cool, though. So, do I get discounts and shit?"

"Nigga, you ain't even started work yet and you tryna get discounts. Type of shit is that?"

The whole ride to his house, we talked, and he was actually cool as hell. He told me him and Jakira were twins, and I wouldn't have guessed that shit.

I pulled up to his house and got out with him. He looked over at me like he ain't know I was gon' come in. I wasn't a damn chauffeur. Wish I would be sitting my ass in the car while this nigga got ready.

JaKolby used his key to get in the house, and somebody was blasting music in the living room. He pointed out where I could go sit, but I followed the music I was being nosey as fuck. When I walked in, I saw Jakira sitting on a stool in front of an easel and canvas. She was painting a picture of a woman's silhouette, and she had a big ass afro. The shit was cold as fuck, and I wanted to buy it to put in my store.

I was sitting on the couch for all of ten minutes before she finally noticed I was there, and she jumped so hard she almost fell off the stool. I was dying laughing, and she looked at me with her lips twisted up, and that's when I noticed her sexy ass dimples.

"How the hell did you get in here? You can't just be poppin' up in people's homes."

"Relax, I brought Kolby home. He upstairs changing so we can go to work." I nodded my head toward the stairs, and she looked at me like she didn't believe me.

"And what kind of work is that?" She put her hands on her small hips, and my eyes went straight to her camel toe.

"I'm opening a clothing store in a few weeks over on Western. You gotta stop through when I have my grand opening." She relaxed and put her arms down at her sides.

"Sorry about that, I'm just not tryna see my brother in no kinda trouble, that's all."

"I feel you. But ay, real shit, that picture dope as fuck. You sellin' it?"

"You think so?" Her face lit up as she looked back at it. "I don't sell my paintings, though; this is just a hobby."

"You should. I'll buy it and hang it up in the store. Just think about it. No matter the price, I want that. And, I always get what I want."

She looked around nervously and cleared her throat. "So, if I said it was five hundred dollars, you would buy it?"

"Hell yeah, that ain't shit."

"Aite, I'm ready." Kolby came downstairs dressed in some jeans and a graphic tee, and he even shaped his little stubble up on his face.

"Let's go. Think about what I said," I said to Jakira before I turned to leave.

I walked out with Kolby behind me, and I felt Jakira staring at me. I was right, because when I turned around, she was looking out of the window.

We rode to the store, and I kept getting calls from my employees because they were sitting outside. I wasn't trusting these niggas with a key to my shit just yet. I had cameras everywhere, but I didn't want people to even think about trying me right now.

"This shit nice as hell." Kolby followed me to the back, and I opened the back door for the trucks.

"Imma show you this one time. I hope you a fast learner, or yo ass gon' be in the unemployment line." I grabbed the smartphones I had for the store inventory and showed him how to check everything in. I checked the shit at the door because if my shit wasn't right, these niggas was gon' be driving right the fuck back to the warehouse to get the rest of my shit.

Kolby caught on quick, so I left him to finish checking the merch in while I showed everybody else where I wanted stuff set up. It took up four hours to get everything set up on the floor, and in the backroom. This shit was looking nice, and I could wait to take the cloth off the windows.

I paid everybody four hundred dollars each and they all left, except for Kolby. I locked the door and waved him to follow me to the office. He made sure the back door was locked, and that was something even I forgot to check.

I pulled a sack of weed out of my pocket and gave Kolby two swishers to break down. We both sat back smoking, and I was in my own thoughts. My mind drifted off to Jakira, so I decided to pick his brain.

"So, what's yo' peoples story. Who all stay in that house?" He sat up straight and put his blunt out in the ashtray.

"It's just me and Kira; that was our mother's house, but she passed like six years ago from cancer. Ever since then, it's just been us two, and we take care of each other. Now, look… I see the way y'all been looking at each other, and that's all cool and shit, but don't play with my sister. I know you a female, but I won't hesitate to fade you over that one."

"Nigga… I will beat yo' ass. Don't let this lil' size fool you, bro. My hands is nice."

"Aite, chill. I ain't tryna fight and have yo' big ass brothers tryna kill me and shit."

"Nah, it's me you gotta worry about. Better ask 'bout me, youngin.'" I put my blunt out, and stood up. "Let's go."

We walked out the office and walked to the front of the store. I had my gun out as I set the alarm and locked the door, and Kolby was lookin' at me crazy.

"Fuck wrong with you?"

"Nothing… we good, boss lady. I don't want no smoke." He put his hands up in mock surrender and walked in front of me.

"Nigga, put yo' hands down, acting like I'm taking yo' punk ass hostage or something." We laughed and got into the car. I put my seatbelt on, and Kolby turned to look at me. I knew he was about to start with some bullshit.

"You cocky as fuck. You know you not a nigga, right?"

"I know exactly who the fuck I am. What's yo' point, you tryna see me in the gloves?"

He scoffed and made the 'yeah right' face. "Destini, you cool as fuck, g, but I wouldn't take it easy on you in the ring."

"Bet it up then, I'll set it up tomorrow."

I was gon' have fun knocking him the fuck out. People always underestimated me because I was a little on

97

the shorter side at 5'4, and since I'm a female, they didn't think I was a threat. We were gon' see about that, though.

I dropped Kolby off and headed home so I could lay my ass down. When I made it home, I saw Tiffany's car parked in front and was instantly irritated. She got out her car when I pulled up, and she waited outside of my car.

"You know better than to be poppin' up at my crib, fuck you want?" I got out and slammed my door shut. She was aggy as fuck.

"How could you do this to us? You're just going to walk away after I gave you a year of my life?!" Tiffany was crying, and I just stared at her until she was done. Tiffany had hella potential, but she was lazy as hell and thought I was gon' fund her damn life. I tried to get the bitch to work at the daycare, and she was talkin' 'bout she don't even have kids, so why would she watch somebody else's kids? Had to tell the bitch I ain't have no damn kids either, so fuck I look like taking care of her ass?

"Look, this shit ain't working for me no mo'."

"Why? Why all of a sudden?" She sucked her tears up real quick and had her hands on her hips.

"I'm tired of yo' mooching ass, na get the fuck away from my crib before you see another side of me, for real." I kept my *other* life away from Tiffany, just for the simple fact I ain't know if I could trust her ass. She thought I owned the clubs and shit with my brothers, so I let her ass keep thinking that.

"You just gon' dump me and that's it? What am I supposed to do?"

"Go get a fuckin' job, I don't care!" I yelled behind me as I walked in the house and locked the door. I watched her kicked my car, then stomp over to hers and pull off. Next time I saw her ass, I was knocking her the fuck out for kickin' my shit.

Chapter Eleven

Dezmund "Dez"

"Wright! You got a visitor, come on." I sat up on my bunk and slipped my feet into my Nike slides.

"Who is it?" I walked next to him toward the door, and was giving head nods to the people who spoke to me.

"I don't know, boss man, they just told me to come get you. Now, you know I gotta cuff you before we go out here." He looked nervous, but I just turned around so he could put the handcuffs on. I knew he was doing his job, so I wasn't gon' trip. We walked out the thick security doors, and down a long hall until we got to the private visiting rooms. When I walked in and saw Ivan sitting across from Detective Normal, I was confused as fuck, but I knew it wasn't good.

"Good afternoon, Mr. Wright. I can see my presence is a bit shocking for you." She held her hand out, and I just looked at it and sat down next to Ivan.

He cleared his throat and fixed his tie before he spoke. "You called me saying you wanted to speak to my client, so let's get down to business."

"Of course." She took two files out of her bag and set them on the table. "Now, these are two homicide cases I happen to be investigating. And, do you know what these two have in common, Mr. Pillar?"

"Humor me," Ivan said and leaned back in his chair.

"In both of these cases, the finger is pointed at one person. Karter Wright." When she mentioned Karter's name, I was ready to strangle her ass in here.

"Now, Dezmund." Detective Normal turned her attention to me now. "I'm sure we both know your wife isn't capable of murdering not one, but *two* people. But, we both know who is capable, isn't that right?"

"I don't think I'm following you, officer," I said smartly as I watched her face turn red.

"Detective."

"My bad."

"So, you have about a week left in here. It would be a shame for you to go home, just for you wife to get sent to here. I see she's pregnant, congratulations." This bitch was making it real hard for me to keep her alive.

"Well, I think this little meeting is over, Detective, have a great day." Ivan stepped in, and Detective Normal just smiled, nodded her head, and grabbed her files to leave. When she walked out the door, Ivan pulled his phone out and was typing away. "I'm going to go through on that harassment suit; at least then, she'll get taken off the case."

"I need to get out of here like now, I need to see my wife."

"You should approve her to come see you."

"I don't want my fuckin' pregnant wife in this hellhole, period."

"You got six days left—"

"I want to be out of here tonight."

"I- I'll see what I can do." I stood up and knocked on the glass so the CO could come take me back to my cell.

As soon as I made it in my cell, I pulled the cover down for privacy and got my phone out. I Facetimed Karter, and she picked up with her beautiful face dripping with sweat, looking like a melting Hershey's bar. Just looking at my wife's face, I calmed down instantly.

"Hey baby, what's wrong?"

"Nothing," I lied. "I just wanted to see your face. Let me see your belly." She laughed and turned the camera around, and it was facing the mirror in her studio. Karter's was still small, but you could tell she had a little baby bump.

"Ay, you need to eat some more, shouldn't you be bigger than that?" She turned the camera around, and her face told how annoyed she was.

"Give me a minute, Tori." She walked to her office, and I saw her close the door. "For your fuckin' information, I gained ten pounds, and my doctor said I'm growing fine. And, I eat so freaking much my cheeks hurt, so don't tell me what the hell I need to do."

"I was just making sure; calm down, Karter. We don't need you getting worked up."

"If you were here, you would see that I'm doing everything I'm supposed to." Her eyes started watering, and she was crying just like that. This pregnancy had her all fucked up, and we weren't even halfway there yet.

"Come on, baby, stop. I'm gon' have some surprises set up for you when you get home. Then, call me when you get done with the last thing, ok?"

She wiped her eyes and was smiling. "Ok, I got to go back out there, but I love you, King, and I'll talk to you later."

"I love you more, Queen." She disconnected the call, and I went right to sending texts out to get this stuff taken care of. Dame said him and Melodee were going to take care of things, and I was glad she was gon' help him because that nigga would fuck some shit up.

I laid back in my bed and stared at the picture Karter sent me the other day. She had just woke up, her hair was all over the place, and she was wearing a little pink, silk gown. Looking at this had me missing waking up to her. I couldn't wait to rub her stomach, man; this shit didn't feel real. Like, she really carrying a piece of me inside of her.

My thoughts switched over to what Detective Normal was talking about. I can't have her tryna lock Karter up, and I definitely wasn't coming back in this bitch, or any other prison. I went to my contacts and sent a text out to Dame.

Me: You right, our hands gon' get dirty

Dame: Heard you… see you soon

Hopefully, Ivan was gon' come through for me, and they were gon' see me sooner than they thought.

Chapter Twelve

Karter

"Ok, I'm ready." Tori was looking at me smiling, and I was trying to ignore her.

"So, you just gon' act like you're not bipolar right now?"

"Leave me alone, it's this baby."

She laughed, and we got back to going over a stand I wanted to teach the Divas. With summer approaching, I wanted to get us in some competitions. The girls were looking great together, and you would think they'd all been dancing together for years.

We took a break at one and sat down to see what we were going to eat.

"Ooohhh, let's go to Taurus Flavor. I want a big ass hoagie." Tori agreed, and we both grabbed our purses and headed out. "We can take my car."

Me and Tori were walking to where I parked, and she kept looking across the street. "Do you know her?" I looked to where she discreetly pointed, and I saw my mother standing at the bus stop.

"Yeah, I do. Hold on; you can get inside and start it up. I handed her the key fob, and she got in the passenger side. I waved my mother over to me and crossed the street. She looked like she had been crying, and I could tell she lost a bunch of weight since I last saw her a few months ago.

"Hi, Karter. I just wanted to speak with you, please."

"Well, I'm my way to go get some food, so..."

"I understand." She put her head down, and for some reason, I started feeling bad.

"Come on, did you eat already?"

"No," she said in a small whisper.

We got in my car, and I drove the short drive to the restaurant. My mom looked nervous when I asked what she wanted, but she ordered a small turkey hoagie. Shit, she could act like she wasn't starving if she wanted to.

"I'll take a double supreme steak, no onions, and add some pickles. Two waters, two bags of barbecue chips, a cheesecake, and a chocolate and strawberry mixed shake." The other people in there were looking at me crazy as I put my order in, and Tori was laughing.

"That's some fat shit, Kay."

"I'm eating for two, shut up."

Once our food was ready, I dropped Tori back up at the studio and told her I'd be back later. I drove to Big Mama's house since I had yet to rent it out, and I for damn sure wasn't taking her to the home where Dez and I lived. She looked around in amazement at all the work we had done. We sat at the dining table with our food, and I gave her a water and a bag of chips. We pretty much ate in silence, and when we were both done, I decided to get right to the point.

"So, why are you here?"

"I just want to start over. Give me a chance to make up with you, or at least a chance to be a grandmother." She looked down at my tiny baby bump, and out of habit, I rubbed it.

"Why should I? Where are you staying?" Just by looking at her, I could tell she wasn't taking good care of herself.

"In a shelter. I just want to be there for you. I missed you much, but I did it to keep you safe. Your fath— Kevin was really messed up back then. If I didn't get you away, there's no telling what he would've done. I took all the abuse I did so that he wouldn't hit you. I'm not trying to get sympathy. I'm just trying to lay it all out on the table."

I was fighting back my tears as she spoke, because I remember the abuse she was talking about. I used to hide in my closet while Kevin beat my mother's ass. She used to beg him to stop, and he wouldn't until I couldn't hear her screaming anymore. One day, I found her unconscious in the middle of the floor, and I thought she was dead.

My vision was getting blurred from the tears that were threatening to fall, and I tried to blink them away. "You should've called, wrote a letter, or something. Do you plan on getting a job?"

"Yeah, I've been looking. It's hard finding something that'll work with the hours of the shelter."

I looked at her and silently prayed that I didn't regret what I was about to do. "Look, you can stay here, and I might be able to get you a job working at my husband's daycare. You will pay rent, and the first time I get a late notice from any utility company, I'm putting you out. Understand?"

I stood up to leave, and I gave her the spare key that was in the lock box in the house. This was definitely my good deed for the month. Hell, maybe next month too. I helped her go get her clothes from wherever she was hiding them, and even took her to Target to get some other things she needed. I didn't know what I was expecting to get outta this, but I just hoped it was good.

By the time I made it home, it was past nine o'clock, and this was the time I usually made it home from practice. I walked into the house, and there were white and red rose petals everywhere. I forgot about Dez's little surprise as I followed the trail to the bedroom, and into the bathroom. The jacuzzi tub was set, and there were bubbles filled to the rim. I smelled my lavender bubble bath and stripped out of my clothes quickly. When I lowered my body into the water, the jets behind me massaged my back, and it felt so good.

I laid in the bath until my body was pruned. Then, I let the water out and went to the shower so I could wash my body off.

When I was done, I brushed my teeth before I went back to the bedroom, and slipped one of Dez's t-shirts on. I was exhausted, so I laid down and was asleep in seconds.

***

I was in a good sleep, drooling and all, when I felt someone touch my stomach.

"Aahh!" I jumped up and my heart was beating out of my chest as I stared into my husband's face. "Dezmund, oh my God, what are you doing here?" He was sitting next to me, so I jumped up and climbed on his lap. I was holding his neck so tight, I was surprised he could breathe.

He pulled back a little bit and planted a kiss on my lips. I kissed him back and stuck my tongue in his mouth. He groaned and smacked me on my ass.

"Girl, you better stop. I need a shower first, then Imma get all up in that. Yo ass don't follow directions, though. The letter said call me when you're done."

"I'm sorry, I fell asleep. That bath was everything after the crazy day I had."

"What happened?" His face got serious, and I shook my head as I climbed off his lap to go pee.

"Relax, it's nothing bad. Well, not really." He followed behind me and was sitting on the sink as I peed.

"Keep going."

"My mom showed up at the studio, and we talked." I finished, so I wiped and flushed the toilet. I went to my side of the sink since he was sitting on his, and washed my hands. "I agreed to let her stay in Big Mama's house, and maybe she can get a job at the daycare."

"Doing what? What type of background do she got? I can't have nobody with no kind of felonies working around these people kids."

"Well, do a freaking background check. I'm sure she's no worse than Jazz, or did you even do a background check on her?" We were still standing in the bathroom, but I stomped out to go lay in the bed, and he was right behind me.

"I thought we were past that shit, Karter. Don't bring old shit into our marriage, bae."

"I'm going back to sleep, Dezmund. Enjoy your shower." I turned my back toward him and closed my eyes until I heard him go into the bathroom and close the door.

This baby had my emotions all over the place, and I started crying.

I heard the bathroom door fly open and tried to suck my tears up. I couldn't explain why I was crying, so I didn't want him to ask me.

"Bae, I'm sorry. I ain't mean to come at you like that. Yo, why you crying, Bugs?" I shrugged my shoulders and wiped my eyes.

He had a towel wrapped around his waist, and he climbed into the bed behind me. I was trying not to focus on the monster that was poking my butt as Dez wrapped his arm around me, and pulled me closer to him.

"You mad at me, baby?" he asked in my ear as his cool breath sent chills down my spine

I shook my head no as he laid a gentle kiss on the nape of my neck and made his way to the front. Before I knew it, the shirt I had on was on the floor, and Dez had my nipple in his mouth. They were sensitive, so it was a little painful at first, but when he spread my legs with his knees and entered me slowly, the only thing I felt was pleasure.

Dez put my legs on his shoulders and sped his pace up. I knew that slow shit wasn't going to last long… it had been years, let Dez tell it.

"Ahhh shit!" I screamed out as I was cumming all over his pole, and he stopped abruptly and looked down at me.

"Did I hurt the baby?" His eyes were wide, and he looked scared. I had to hold my laugh in because he was really scared.

"No, keep going, Dez." He flipped us over and had me on top of him, like this was going to be better. Dez made love to me until we were both breathing like two slaves that had been running on the underground railroad all night.

Dez fell asleep first, and I didn't even mind his snoring; that's how much I missed him. I laid on his chest and listened to his heartbeat until I went back to sleep. I swear, I hoped this wasn't a dream, or I was gonna be pissed.

****

When I woke up the next morning, I was the only one in bed and jumped up to check the house. I smelled him on the pillows, so I knew I wasn't going crazy and imagining shit.

I walked downstairs, and Dez was walking in the house at the same time. He had a bag from Flapjacks in his hands. He smiled when he saw me, and he met me at the entry of the kitchen to give me a kiss. I ran to the bathroom that was on the main floor and emptied my bladder before I had an accident on the floor. I washed my hands and went back to the kitchen, where I saw Dez setting up our spots at the table. He got me some strawberry flapjacks, turkey sausage patties, hash browns, and a vegetarian omelet. This was me and Dez's favorite spot to go, and I always got the same thing.

"So, how did you do it?" I was dying to know what the hell he did to get out, and why he didn't do it earlier.

"Do what?" I gave him the 'really nigga?' look, and he chuckled. "I still got a few connections that I try not to use often." He took a bite of his waffles and looked at me, smirking. I thought he would've put his grill back in by now, but he didn't and I was loving it. "Why you over there raping me with your eyes?"

"Because you look good, bae. You about to be dirty thirty next week, my old man."

"Ain't shit old about me, baby. I saw the way you was walking when you came down the stairs."

"Stop playing so much, goofball." We ate our food as we talked about the baby, and Dez's face was lit up. I was glad he was just as excited as I was about the baby, not that he had a choice anyway.

"When can we find out what we having?"

"At my 20-week appointment. Do you want to do something cute for the reveal?"

"For who, Karter?"

I kissed my teeth and threw a napkin at him. "You just gotta take the fun outta everything."

"We don't need to do all that extra stuff right now. We can do it big for the baby shower shit."

"Fine, well we don't have that long to go." I cleaned the table off and went upstairs to get dressed for the day. I didn't have any plans, and I was hoping Dez didn't either because I wanted to just spend time together, just him and I. That was short lived as everybody popped up late in the afternoon with bottles and weed. I couldn't partake in the festivities, but it was fun being around everyone again. Destini brought the guy JaKolby with her, and they went back and forth all night; you would've sworn he was one of their siblings. I thought it was hilarious because Destini finally ran into somebody that was gon' go back and forth with her.

Everybody left around midnight, and Dez and I showered together before we cuddled up in bed. I was tired, and Dez was too damn drunk. I wasn't letting him nowhere near my kitty tonight.

Chapter Thirteen

Melodee

"Damn, you don't hear me talkin' to you, Mel?"

"Huh? I'm sorry. What you say?" We were in the car going home after leaving Dez and Karter's house, and I was zoned out, looking out the window.

"Fuck you over there thinkin' bout?" Dame asked, peeking over at me before he put his eyes back on the road.

"Nothing."

"You better say sumn befo' I think you was dreamin' about a nigga and fuck you up."

"Damien, you ain't gon' do shit. And I'm not thinking about no nigga, so shut the hell up."

"Ok, so talk to me." He pulled into the driveway of our home, and we got out the car.

"I need something to do with my life." Dame unlocked the front door and let me walk in first.

"I ain't following you, baby."

"Never mind, let me go shower." I walked in our adjoining bathroom, and Dame went to the bathroom down the hall to shower. When I was finished, my thoughts were still all over the place, so I hurriedly got dressed in my pajamas so I could talk to Dame. He had just walked in the room, and he was rubbing oil into his beard.

"I'm the damn bum of the crew! Everybody got businesses and shit, and what do I have? A car," I blurted, and Dame stopped what he was doing and started dying laughing. I mean, he was bent over holding his damn stomach, and I wanted to punch him in his big ass lips.

"I'm sorry, that was funny as hell, baby. You be running the club and shit, though, and you got me. What more could you want?"

"I *run* the club, I don't own it. That's y'all shit."

"I'll add yo' name on there tomorrow, it's cool."

"No, I don't want yo' fuckin' club. I'm tired of being there anyway."

"Ay, don't be turning yo' nose up to my shit, like you wasn't in there shaking yo' ass."

"I just don't want it." I rolled my eyes, and Dame sat next to me, pulling me onto his lap. He thought he was slick; he always did this when he wanted some ass, and it wasn't happening tonight.

"So, what you want then, baby? Whatever you want, I got you." He was rubbing my booty, and I almost got sucked into his shit.

"You saying whatever you think I wanna hear." He threw me off his lap, damn near making me fall onto the floor, and laid on his side of the bed.

"I ain't no goofy ass nigga. If I tell you some shit, I mean it. Fuck would I just say some shit for if I ain't mean it? I don't talk to hear myself talk, bro!" His yellow ass was turning red as he threw my decorative pillows on the floor.

"You need to relax, Damien. Ain't nobody called you a goofy."

"Naw, you on some bullshit. I was gon' give you some dick, now you ain't getting shit." Now, it was my turn to laugh as I got comfortable in bed and turned my back to him. Ain't nobody have time for Dame's mess right now.

In the middle of the night, I felt Dame tryna slide my shorts to the side, and I popped the shit out of his hands. Now, he was moping around the house like he lost his best friend. Instead of acknowledging his foolishness, I quickly got dressed and left out the house. I heard Dame yelling behind me, asking where I was going, but I didn't answer. I honestly didn't know where the hell I was going. I knew Karter was gon' be locked in the house with Dez being nasty, so I definitely wasn't going there. Destini was gon' try to get me to do some damn work, and I definitely wasn't doing that shit.

Instead of wasting my gas, I went to the mall and did some retail therapy. Dame thought I was playing, but I really felt like I wasn't doing nothing with my life. I mean, I was young, only twenty-six years old, but I felt like I should be building for my future or something. I was gonna get it together soon, just watch.

***

Dame: Fuck you at?

I read Dame's message and put my phone back in my pocket. I decided to go to the movies after swiping my card all day, and I saw *Justice League*. When it was over, I slowly gathered the bags that I had and started toward the door. My phone was ringing nonstop in my pocket, and when I tried to get it, I ended up dropping a couple of items on the floor.

"Shit!"

"You need help?" I looked up to see my ex, Rodney, standing over me.

"Not today, Satan," I whispered as I threw my clothes back in the bag and stupid up. "No, thank you." He grabbed my arm when I turned to walk away, and I was about to show my ass in here.

"Aye Mel, fuck is this nigga?" Dame came stomping toward me, and I just knew the devil was having a field day with my ass right now. I looked back at Rodney, and he was sneering at Dame. If his ass knew what was good for him, he better go have that attitude in his car.

"Naw, who the fuck is you, nigga?"

Dame took a step forward, and I jumped in front of him before he became the next damn Wright in jail.

"Bae, come on, it's too many people in here. Let's just go... please." The look Dame gave me sent chills down my spine. He didn't say a word as he took my bags out my hand, giving Rodney a look that would have his mama picking out her Sunday's best before we left out. He followed behind me to where I parked my car and literally threw my shit in the backseat. I was about to say something smart, but Dame grabbed me by my collar and pushed me against my car. It wasn't hard, but I could tell he wanted to do more.

"Why the fuck you wasn't answerin' yo' phone? And I gotta see you with this nigga at the movies and shit? You cheating on me with that nigga?" Dame was so close in my face, I felt his beard tickling my nose.

"First of all, you better back up like three feet and talk to me like you got some sense."

"Yeah aite, go straight to the crib, Mel. I swear, you don't wanna test me right now." He walked away, and I just shrugged and got in my car. I wasn't going straight nowhere, tho. He was gon' wait until I got my damn ice cream.

I pulled in our driveway almost thirty minutes later, and Dame was sitting on the porch smoking. He watched me as I got all my bags out and went inside the house. By the time I made it to the bedroom, he was right on my heels, breathing hard as fuck.

"Can I help you, Damien?" I asked, turning around to give him the same crazy ass look he was giving me.

"Yeah *Melodee*, you can help me by telling me where the fuck you been?"

"Well, you can clearly see where I've been." I smartly replied as I pointed to the bags I had sitting on the floor.

"So, why the fuck you ain't answer? I'm thinkin' sumn' happened to yo nappy headed ass. Got me out here like a stalker and shit."

"Oh, now you care about me, huh?"

"The fu— man, you know I love yo' ass. What you talkin' bout, bae?" His face softened, and he tried to reach for my hand, but I snatched it away.

"When I told you what was bothering me, you thought it was sooo funny. So, don't try to be this caring mothafucka now. Ugh, just forget it, Damien." I stormed in the bathroom and closed the door behind me. I just wanted to take a shower and relax my mind.

I know I probably looked crazy, but shit, I felt crazy too. After all these years, I was finally letting my father get to me. Just because I decided that college wasn't for me, I was basically disowned and told that I would never amount to nothing without a college education. For that reason, I hadn't seen or talked to my parents since I graduated high school. I mean, they act like I was going to sell my ass on the corner. I just didn't want to do more school after the twelve years I just finished.

Thinking about my parents always made me sad. Like, how could somebody just not care to check on their only child, to see if they're ok, or just to tell them that they love 'em?

I was so into my thoughts, I didn't hear Dame when he came into the bathroom. The cold air hit me when he snatched the curtains open, and I jumped so hard I almost fell.

"You don't hear me talkin' to you? Yo, you crying?" Dame pulled me in his arms and sat on the toilet with my naked, wet body in his lap. "You wanna talk about it?" I shook my head no, and he didn't say anything else. Once I was done with my little breakdown, Dame stood up and placed me back on my feet.

125

The shower was still going, so I stepped in and watched as Dame stripped out of his clothes as well. He joined me in the shower and took his time washing me with my favorite lavender body wash. This was new for Dame, to be all gentle with me. Any other day, I could barely get him to scratch my back. Now, he had done washed me from the top of my head, down the crack of my ass without me saying anything. When he was done, we stepped out the tub, and went into the room, where I rubbed myself down with my moisturizer.

For the rest of the night, we cuddled in bed until I drifted off to sleep. I hoped he don't try to bring this up again tomorrow, but knowing Damien, he was.

***

I woke up the next morning, and Dame ass was sitting on the side of the bed staring at me. "What the hell is yo creep ass doing, Dame?"

"Shit, yo ass wasn't breathing, I had to check on you. Yo jack been blowing up all morning, too."

"What time is it?"

"Time for you to get up and tell me what the hell going on with you. I left you alone last night because I ain't really know what to do with you crying and shit. So, talk to me, baby." I sat up in the bed and decided to tell Dame everything.

"Bae, fuck them old muhfuckas, you know yo' man gon' support you through everything. Whatever you want to do, I got you. We can get up today and get shit moving. Come on, get up and take care of that dragon breath." He playfully smacked my thigh, and we both laughed. I handled my hygiene and got dressed for the day. Dame was handling business on the phone while I checked my messages. Most of them were from Destini, so I called her back instead of texting.

"Damn, Melly Mel. You just gon' ignore me like that, bro?"

"Nigga, I was sleep. What you want?"

"Wright Spot is officially done, and I need you to get the grand opening set up for me."

"Who the hell do you think I am, Destini? I do not work for you." I was just giving her shit; I knew I was gon' help.

"Come on, how much you gon' charge me, man?"

"I'll have my people contact yo' people and let you know."

"You ain't got no damn people. Bye, g." I laughed as I walked downstairs and grabbed a muffin out the kitchen.

"So, what's the verdict?"

"What you think about me getting into event planning?"

Dame nodded his head in approval. "I think it's dope as fuck. You know I don't know shit about that, but I'll do what I can."

"Ok, because I got my first client and you gotta help me."

"Let's go eat first, then we can handle that."

"You read my mind and my stomach. I don't know what I thought this little ass muffin was gon' do for me."

"Knowing you be eatin' like a grown ass man, bro."

"Shut yo ass up, Damien." We left out and got in his car.

I was excited for this new journey, and I already knew it was gon' take off. My parties were always lit, and people loved me.

Chapter Fourteen

Destini

Looking around the store, my chest was poked out like a muhfucka. Everything was done, and I couldn't wait to open the doors officially.

"My sis pickin' me up, so I don't need a ride today," Kolby said as we did one last walkthrough of the store.

"Aw, yeah? When she gon' be here?" The look on his face had me bent over laughing.

"Ay, Imma forget you a chick and knock yo' ass out one day."

"I keep tellin' you come on and make my day, bro, it ain't sweet over here." The front door chimed, and we both turned our attention in that direction. I smiled, and Kolby playfully pushed me to the side.

"Hey y'all, it looks nice in here," Jakira said in her little squeaky voice.

"Thanks, I just need that painting right here and it's gon' be complete." I pointed to the empty space on the wall where I was planning to put the picture, and she smiled.

"I didn't think you were serious."

"I mean everything I say, baby." Jakira was smiling shyly at me and started playing with her hands. Kolby cleared his throat, and we both turned to look at him. "What, nigga?"

"Just get her number and come on. I'm tired as hell." We exchanged numbers and all left out together. Once I made sure everything was locked up and the alarm was set, I got in the car and headed over to my girl, Lovely, so she could do my hair. I was tired of this blonde and wanted my shit dyed black again.

When I pulled up to the shop, it was packed with cars everywhere. For a Friday afternoon, I already knew I was probably gon' be in this bitch all night.

"Dest!" I turned around in the parking lot and saw Tiffany walking up to me.

"Fuck you want?" I didn't even try to hide my irritation. I wanted her to know how pissed I was.

"That's how you gon' talk to me? Really?"

"G, you got five seconds to tell me what you want."

"I want US, Dest. How could you just give up after everything we been through?"

"What the hell have we been through? Not a mothafucking thing. Next time you see me, keep it pushing."

"I'm not going anywhere!" I waved her off and tried to count to ten so I could keep my hands to myself. Every time I saw her, I thought about the bitch kickin' my ride, and I wanted to redo this parking lot with her ass.

"Bye, man." I went into the shop and was greeted by everybody in there.

"Hey girl, I almost forgot you was coming," Lovely said as her client got up to sit under the dryer.

"I'm getting rid of this blonde. I need to be more incognito."

"I got you, come on and sit down."

Lovely did my hair, and it took all of an hour and a half to finish. As always, she got me right, and I tipped her extra before I left. When I walked to my car, I saw I had four flats, and I was seeing red. I called my brothers and them niggas ain't answer, so I tried calling Mel since I knew Karter was in practice.

"You don't never call me this much in one day. What the hell you want?"

"I need a favor. This bitch, Tiffany, slashed my tires. I'm at Lovely's shop."

"Huuuuhhh, aite. Here I come. You owe me some gas money too."

"Fuck outta here." I smacked my lips and hung up the phone. It took her 15 minutes to get to me and when she pulled up, she was wearing sweatpants and had her hair wrapped up in a ponytail.

"Where this hoe live at?" This why I fucked with Melodee; she was always ready, and always been that way.

"Right over on 87th street, I'll show you." We pulled up to Tiffany's neighborhood, and there were a few people outside. The sun had just gone down, but I spotted Tiffany's loud mouth ass in a crowd.

"Oh shit, Tiff!" Her sister tried to warn her that I was coming, and by time she turned around, I was punching her in her shit.

"Aahhh, my eye! Somebody help me! Tierra, get her off me!" She was screaming and flopping around on the ground like somebody was killin' her ass, and I damn near wanted to.

"Tierra better stay her ass over there unless she wanna share an ass whooping with her sister!" I heard Melodee say from behind me as I tried to stomp Tiffany's ears together. I kept whooping her ass until I got tired, then we walked back to the car like nothing ever happened.

"So... did you call a tow truck?"

"Yeah, just take me to the crib."

I wasn't mad about the tires, but my Benz was my favorite car. Melodee pulled up to my place, and I thanked her before I got out. This bitch ruined my damn mood, and I was ready to go back and stomp her ass some more. Instead, I took a shower and laid my ass down. Jakira crossed my mind and I was gon' hit her up, but I changed my mind about it and went to sleep. I was definitely hitting her up tomorrow, though.

Chapter Fifteen

Dezmund "Dez"

The smell of some good ass food woke me up, and I rolled outta bed to go see what my baby was cooking up. I been home a week, and she had been cooking every day. She was acting like she was tryna get a ring, and we married already. After I pissed and handled my hygiene, I went downstairs to see my mama cooking, and Karter was sitting on a stool looking sexy as well with a yellow sundress on.

"Look at my two favorite women. Good morning." I reached Karter first, and she was cheesing hard as I leaned down to kiss her soft lips and rubbed her stomach. Mama stopped running around the kitchen long enough so I could give her a kiss on the cheek, and she finished cooking.

"Happy birthday, baby!" Damn. It's crazy, I forgot my own damn birthday. I been busy tryna make sure we stayed outta fuckin' jail, and I wasn't thinkin' 'bout nothing else.

"Thanks, baby. Why you dressed so early?"

"We find out what we having today, duuuh, so hurry up and get dressed." It was my time to start cheesin' now. I couldn't wait until Karter had the baby. I'd feel complete then. Even though I ain't know shit about taking care of a baby, I knew we was gon' be good.

"Aite, what about my food, though? I'm hungry as hell. My bad, Ma." She gave me a look like she was about to swell my lip up, so I just went to get dressed. When I came back, Karter rushed me out the door, and we headed to the doctor's office.

"I'm so excited. I don't even care what we have, as long as it's healthy." Karter was glowing, and I swear my wife was the most beautiful pregnant woman ever. I couldn't wait until her stomach got bigger and she had that lil' waddle pregnant women get.

"I need two boys first, then we can try for a girl or two."

"How many damn kids you tryna have, Dezmund?"

"Shiiiiit, a few; gotta be fruitful, baby." We arrived at the clinic, and I helped her out the car. Once she was checked in, we sat in the corner and waited for her to be called. My phone rang, and I stepped outside to answer it. It was Ivan, and I hoped he was calling with some good news.

"Talk to me, Iv."

"How are you feeling this morning, Mr. Wright?"

"What the hell you got for me, Ivan? I'm at the doctor with my wife, so speak fast."

"Apparently, there was a break in the case and they have a witness to the murder of Jazmyne Fields. They didn't say who it is or what they witnessed, but they did say it was a woman who was seen leaving the house."

Fuck!

"Aite, thanks Ivan. I'll get back with you later." I hung up and took a deep breath before I went back inside with Karter. She was reading a baby magazine and stopped to look over at me before she continued reading. I tried to look as unbothered as I could, but I was pissed on the inside. I knew I was gon' have to kill this bitch, Detective Normal. I didn't know what her issue was with my family, but I knew she wasn't gonna just drop the shit.

"Karter Wright?" She was finally called to the back, and we followed the nurse to the room. She took her blood pressure and weight, and I just sat in the chair against the wall.

"The doctor will be in shortly." When the door closed, Karter looked over at me, and I tried to force a smile so she wouldn't start to worry.

"What's wrong, Dez?"

"Nothing, baby. Why you ask that?"

"Ever since you got that phone call, your face has been balled up."

Damn, so much for playing the shit off. "I'll tell you later, let's just enjoy this moment. We about to see our baby." She opened her mouth to say something else, but the doctor walked in and I wanted to thank him. I didn't know how I felt about another nigga all up in my wife's pussy, though. I was gon' have to talk to her 'bout this shit later.

"Alright, everything is looking good. You bloodwork came back normal. Go ahead and lay back so we can get a look at the little one." I brought my chair closer, and the doctor dimmed the lights before he went to the ultrasound machine that was on the other side of the bed. "This gel is going to be a little cold, I apologize."

He put the instrument on her stomach and moved it around. When the little big head alien popped up on the screen, my chest swelled with pride. That was my seed in there moving around. "Baby measurements are looking good, nice and healthy. Do you two want to know the sex?"

"Yes!" we eagerly answered at the same time, causing the doctor to laugh.

"Alright, mommy and daddy. Congratulations on your baby boy."

"Hell yeah!" I jumped up and got closer to the ultrasound monitor, like I knew what the fuck I was looking at.

"Dezmund, sit down. I'm sorry about that." Karter laughed and pulled me back.

"It's absolutely fine, this is a normal reaction. Like I said before, everything looks good with baby, and mommy, continue to eat right and stay hydrated. Make your next appointment for four weeks, and I'll see you then."

"Thanks, doc." I shook his hand, and he walked out the room. I helped Karter out of the bed, and we left after she made her appointment for the next visit.

Karter was typing away on her phone in the passenger seat, and I knew she was telling Mel about the baby. While I was happy as fuck about my son, I needed to get a handle on this bullshit before he made his arrival.

"Bae, what's going on?" Karter's small hand caressing my face snapped me out of my thoughts.

"Nothing, why you ask?"

"I've been talking to you, and you haven't said a word. Who was it that called you back there, Dezmund?"

"Ivan."

"Ok, so what did he say?" I thought long and hard about what I was going to say next. I hadn't told her that I was the one responsible for her death, and I honestly didn't know if I was gon' tell her. Didn't look like I had much of a choice now, though.

"There was a witness in the Jazz murder."

"That's good, then they know I didn't do the shit and can leave us alone about it." I pulled up to our home and saw a few cars parked in the driveway. When I looked over at Karter, she was smiling, so I know she had something to do with this. "Don't be mad; it's your siblings, and I invited Kolby too."

"Ok, but I gotta tell you something."

"Can it wait?" she asked with concern written all over her face.

"No. Ivan said the witness saw a woman leaving Jazz's house the night of her murder."

"Bae, we weren't even in the state. They can't charge me with anything."

"Yeah, but Destini was." Karter gasped, and her hand went over her mouth. "The day we left for Cali, Jazz popped up at the daycare. She told me she was going to press charges on you for beating her ass if I ain't fuck her. I know I probably could've handled it differently, but know I'll do anything to keep you and our son outta harm's way."

"Why didn't you tell me this sooner, Dezmund?!"

"I didn't want you involved."

"Well, look how great that's going," she said sarcastically. She snatched her seatbelt off and turned her body to face me. "So, am I going to be arrested soon or something? Am I gonna have to serve time for your sister,

142

Dezmund? I can't fuckin' believe this!" Karter opened her door and got out, and I was right behind her.

"You not going to jail, Karter. Calm the fuck down before you stress my son out. Imma handle it."

"Of course, you will." She went into the house and went right up the stairs toward the room. All eyes were on me as she slammed the door, and I heard the picture in the hallway fall.

"Well, damn. Happy birthday, bro." Destini had to be the one to speak up. I shook my head and went around dapping everybody up. This was not how I wanted to spend my birthday.

Chapter Sixteen

Karter

I was heated as I paced back and forth in the room. I can't go to jail, I'm tired of dealing with fuckin' police. I just want to get through this pregnancy, and live a happy life. I love Dezmund, I swear I do, but this is becoming too much for me.

Knock! Knock!

I sighed and sat on the ottoman. "Come in!" Ma poked her head in the door before she came all the way in and sat next to me.

"What's going on, Karter baby? Is the baby ok?"

"Yes, he's fine." She smiled big and clapped her hands together.

"Ooohh it's a boy, I'm so excited. So, what's the matter?" I didn't know if she was up to date on what was going on or not, but I wasn't going to be the one to tell her.

"I don't want to bother you with our problems, Ma."

"Ok, well come on and feed granny baby. Food is done, and you know those savages downstairs won't hesitate to eat it all." Ma got up, and I followed her down to the kitchen.

Dez followed me intensely with his eyes around the kitchen, and I did everything to avoid his stare. Him and his damn siblings were on my shit list right now, so I wasn't saying shit to neither one of them.

"Y'all tryna go get this paintball war cracking?" Dame asked once everyone was done eating.

"I'm in," Destini spoke up first, and everyone agreed to go too. I didn't say anything because I wasn't going any damn where. Not like I could participate anyway.

Once the house was back in order, everyone left to get changed, and they agreed to meet in an hour. Melodee and Dame took Ma home, so it was just me and Dez left, and I was still ignoring him. I had my Kindle out, checking for new releases, and Dez took it upon himself to sit next to me.

"Bugs, you got me fucked up if you think you gon' keep ignoring me."

Silence

He snatched my Kindle out of my hand and threw it on the other couch. I forgot how petty my husband could be at times.

"What, Dezmund?" I huffed and looked at him.

"Fuck is you mad for, man? I'm bussin' my ass tryna make sure this shit don't come back to you or my fuckin' sister! I understand you mad, but I did this shit for you, for US! Don't that shit count for something?" Dez jumped up from the couch and stood over me.

"You should've told me! Why wait months after the fact?! If you couldn't trust me with that information, why the hell did you marry me? I can't do this."

"What? You can't do what? Whatever the fuck you thinkin', you better get that shit out yo' big ass head, for real." He was pacing and shaking his head as he glared at me, like I talked about his mama.

"I can't do this! I'm sorry, I'm not some gutta ride or die bitch who don't care about this shit. I fuckin' killed someone, Dezmund! I have another murder being pinned on me, and it feels like the fuckin' walls are closing in on me! All I want to do is have a healthy and normal marriage and pregnancy. Maybe this is a sign that we moved too fast."

"So, because this one little thing pops up, you ready to walk away from me?"

"Little? It's murder, Dezmund! There's nothing *little* about that. Especially the fuckin' time in jail Imma get if I'm convicted. I can't go to jail." I dropped my head in my lap and cried. This shit was stressful as hell, and I just didn't know what to do anymore.

"Karter? Baby, I'm sorry, look at me." He got on his knees in front of me, lifted my head up, and planted a soft kiss on my lips. "Don't leave me, I promise Imma fix it before the baby even gets here…. just don't leave." A lone tear rolled down his cheek and I wiped it for him, then attacked his lips with mine. This baby had my hormones all outta whack; I went from pissed, sad, to horny. Dez didn't seem to mind as he pulled my dress up and rubbed my southern lips with his index finger. He sent a trail of kisses down my body and stopped at my stomach to rub it and kiss it once more before he continued down lower.

"Mmmmm baaaaeeee, shit." The way Dez was eating my pussy, you would swear he was starving to death.

When he flicked his tongue slowly up and down my clit, my legs started to twitch, and I felt myself about to cum.

"This shit taste so good, baby, sweet as fuck. Give me that nut, Karter. Feed me, baby." Just like that, my body responded to him, and I was cumin' so hard I saw my soul float out my body and wave bye to me. When Dez came up, his chin was dripping with my juices, and he didn't bother to wipe it off.

He pulled his pants down, snatched me up off the couch, and turned me around so I was leaned over the back of it. Dez filled me up, and we both moaned out in pleasure as he held my waist and moved in and out me with precision. "Throw that ass back, Kay." I did what he said as he continued his assault on my kitty.

Wap! "Yeah, just like that." He smacked my ass so hard, and I knew it was going to leave a mark. I felt Dez's manhood pulsating inside of me, and I knew he was about to cum. "Aarrggh!" He held himself up so he wouldn't fall on me, then pulled out and sat on the couch.

"Damn bae, I think I got you pregnant again."

"Shut up, stupid." I laughed and playfully hit him in the chest. "Dez, I'm sorry, all this is just...a lot. But, you know I'm not going anywhere, ever. Til' death do us part, baby."

"I already knew you weren't going anywhere, and if you tried to, death was gon' do us part for real because I was gon' kill yo' ass," he spoke so smoothly, like he didn't just threaten my life.

"Ok, I'm going to go shower. Are you going to go paintballing?"

"I thought about it, you tryna ride?" He followed behind me to the bathroom and grabbed what he needed to take a shower.

"Naw, you go ahead and enjoy your birthday, baby. I was actually thinking about going to check on my mom. Don't look at me like that, bae. She's been calling me like crazy, and I think I want to try to work on our relationship. It might be good for the baby to have two grandparents instead of one." I was rambling, trying to get him to see where I was coming from, and he put his hand on my lower back.

"Calm down, baby. It's ok, just be careful if you go, or I could go with you."

"No baby, go celebrate and I'll see you when you get back." We both showered, got dressed, and left out together.

"You better call me when you make it, and when you leave. Don't play with me."

"Yes daddy, have fun." We kissed and both got in our cars to leave.

The ride to see my mother seemed longer than usual, and I was nervous. I hadn't seen her since I brought her here, and even though she called me almost every day, I always made excuses on why I couldn't talk because I didn't know what to say.

"Karter? Hi, come on in. I wasn't expecting company. Why didn't you use your key? Oh Lord, look at your little belly." She opened the door, and I was shocked by her appearance. My mom had gained a little weight and looked like she had been taking care of herself.

"I didn't want to just barge in; this is your place now," I said as I sat down on the couch.

"It's no problem, it's not like I do anything in here. Stop by whenever you want."

"How are you, Mom?"

"I've been doing better, living one day at a time. I've been wanting to do something, and I want to ask can you come with me?"

"What is it?"

"I want to see Big Mama. I need to see where my mother is buried."

My heart dropped to my stomach when those words left her mouth. I couldn't bring myself to go back and see Big Mama after she was buried; it was just too much.

"I- I don't know, I'll let you know where she is, but I can't go."

I stayed there for almost two hours talking, and I only left because I had practice tomorrow. I could say I was feeling good about where this was heading. I just hoped she didn't make me regret this.

Chapter Seventeen

Destini

The last couple weeks had been crazy as I made sure everything was together for the grand opening tomorrow. I don't think I had time to scratch my ass in the last two weeks, let alone get some decent sleep. Another thing I hadn't had time for was Jakira. That's why I was on my way to pull up at her crib to see her. When I parked in front of their house, I sent her a text to see if she was home and waited for her to respond.

Jakira: hey, I'm not doing nothing, watching TV. Wbu?

Me: shit, feel like company?

Jakira: sure

Me: open the door

I got out the car and went to the front door as it opened. Jakira stood there wearing some little ass shorts and a tank top, and her hair was in a bun at the top of her head. She was in rare form, but it was sexy as hell to me.

152

"Hey, I thought you forgot about me or something," she said as she let me inside and closed the door.

"Naw, shit just been crazy for me. You coming to the grand opening tomorrow?"

"Of course, I'll be there. You look… different with black hair, but I like it." She touched the shaved side of my head and smiled.

"'Preciate it, so where bro at?"

"Spending time with my niece, he'll be back later. Did you come for him or me?"

"You, of course. Ya know I had to come see about my future." We got comfortable on the couch, and she resumed the show she was watching on Netflix.

"You ever seen Scandal?" I gave her that 'yeah right' look and she laughed. Even her damn laugh was sexy as hell. I didn't know what she was doing to me, but this shit felt… right. We sat back watching a few episodes of this show, and I ain't gon' lie, but this shit was good as hell. I fucked around watch it at home from the beginning.

When I started getting tired, I stood up so I could get ready to leave. "I gotta get outta here so I can catch up on some sleep and shit, but I'll get with you tomorrow."

"Ok, it was nice seeing you. Maybe next time, you'll take me out instead of Netflix and chill." We shared a laugh as she walked me to the door.

"I got you next week, for real. Shit's crazy right now, but Imma make time for you." I turned around to leave and drove home feeling like a damn fairy how happy I was. I ain't never felt like this about Tiffany or no other bitch, so that's how I knew it was real.

The next morning, I got up early as hell to get dressed so I could go make sure shit was moving how it should be for the grand opening. I had to pick Kolby up, so I grabbed him and the nigga looked half sleep.

"Wake yo' bitch ass up, man. We got work to do."

"Maaan, don't start with that bullshit, it's too early for all that. Fuck was you doing over here yesterday, though? Don't be corrupting my sister, man."

"Stay outta grown folks' business, lil' boy."

Kolby rolled up, and we smoked the whole ride to the store. Everything was looking A1 as hell on the inside, and I had to give Melodee her props. She was there running around, screaming at muhfuckas, but she was getting the job done.

"She fine as hell. I'll take her from Dame, for real," Kolby said lowly so Mel couldn't hear.

"Yeah, and if you try to get at her, Dame gon' beat yo ass black and blue. He don't play 'bout that one."

"I ain't worried 'bout it."

"Yeah, we'll see."

***

"Thank y'all for coming out to support ya girl, I appreciate it. I hope y'all ain't coming just to eat, buy shit some shit too. Ow!" Ma was standing by me and reached over to smack the back of my head, and everyone laughed. Mel handed me some big ass scissors, and I cut the ribbon in that was wrapped around the front. That shit was her idea. I told her ass I just wanted to open the let muhfuckas in. She just had to be fancy with it.

The stored filled up quick, and I got a lot of compliments on the store.

"I'm so proud of my baby. You handled yo' business, and look at all this. Can I wear some of this stuff in here?"

"Nah ma, you stay in Ashley Stewart or wherever you be getting yo' clothes from."

"Don't be a hater." I shook my head at Ma and walked off to mingle with everybody in the building. The DJ was on point, and the entire party was live; only thing that was missing was Jakira.

"It looks good in here." It's crazy; when I start thinking about her, that's when she pops up. I gave her a hug, and she handed me a big gift that was in her hand.

"Thank you, what is this?" I opened the bag and pulled the painting out that I told her I wanted. "Awww shit, it's lit now. Let me go put this in my office until I get something to hang it up with."

She followed me to the back and I put the picture against the wall, then sat behind the desk. I had a stash behind my desk, so I pulled it out and rolled a fat one.

"You smoke?" I asked Jakira as I took a hit.

"Not really. I have before, but I tweak too hard."

"I feel you." I continued to smoke, and she sat in the chair across from me. If this was anybody else, I probably would've had her stretched across my desk, but I wanted more from Jakira so I was gon' chill. I took a few more hits of the blunt and put it out. I stood up, and Jakira followed me back out to where everyone else was.

"It really does look good in here. I see a few pieces I want to grab before I leave," Jakira exclaimed as we walked through the women's section.

"Thanks, ma. I been in overdrive tryna get this done, but let me finish walking around. Enjoy yourself, and if you need anything, let me know." She smiled, showing off those deep dimples, and went right to a rack of clothes.

Dez waved me over to him, so I made it to where he and Karter were sitting. "What's poppin', broski? How my lil' nigga doing in there?" I asked, rubbing Karter's stomach. She slapped my hand away, and I laughed.

"Dez, you better tell your sister stop calling my son a nigga before I knock her out." Karter playfully rolled her eyes, then stood up. "I'm going to make me another plate,

I'm starving." She walked off, and we just shook our heads. I sat in the seat she was occupying and turned my attention to my bro. He still had his eyes on Karter, like she was gon' disappear or some shit.

"Wassup?"

"Shit lookin' nice in here. I'm proud of you, for real. Usually, you be playin' and shit, but you handled yo' business and got the shit done."

"Aaawww shit, you tryna make a real nigga cry in here," I joked and wiped my imaginary tears away.

"See what I mean? Play too damn much. Step outside with me right quick, though." His face got serious, so mine did too as we made our way outside and to his ride. He sparked a blunt up and tried to pass it to me, but I declined.

"I just got done blowing in the back, I can't be slumped in there."

"I feel you. I'm waiting on Dame to bring his ugly ass out here so I ain't gotta repeat myself. But, while we wait, who was shorty that had yo' ass in there skinnin' and grinnin'?"

"Maaaan, fuck outta here, ain't nobody grinnin' and shit," I tried to say to with a straight face, but ended up smilin' anyway. Dez started laughing, and I had to join in. "That's Kolby's sister, man. She bad as hell, ain't she?"

"Aawww shit, let me find out you dun fell in love."

"I ain't all that now, you buggin'."

"My bad, y'all. Almost had to flex Kolby lil' ass for lookin' at Mel. Told the lil' nigga he got a death wish, for real," Dame said as he slid in the backseat. I gave Dez a look, telling him to drop the subject, and he just nodded. Dame's ass play more than me, and I was gon' end up beating his ass out here.

"Aite, few weeks ago, I got a call from Ivan saying they had a witness that saw a woman leavin' Jazz crib the night you murked her. You wanna tell me how you let that happen?"

Fuck!

"It was dark as fuck, ain't no way somebody saw me."

159

"Yeah, they ain't see yo face, but they knew it was a female who did it, and this detective gon' be a pain in my ass."

"We could've been handled that bitch, bro. Me and Dest could've peeled her shit when you were locked up. Shit would be easy sailing right now." Dame spoke up with a mug etched on his face.

"Obviously, you sloppy mothafuckas needed me here because *that* shit should've been smooth sailing, but here we are, having this conversation."

"What's the plan?" I had to say something before these two started going at it. 'Cause I ain't got time to be tryna break these big muhfuckas up.

"I paid a visit to the so-called witness, threw her a few bands, and she agreed to tell them she ain't see shit. Now, the pigs on our payroll claim they been tryna get rid of evidence little by little, but this bitch Normal is determined to put our black asses away for this shit. Karter was cleared because of our alibi, but you two need to think of something before she decides to come pick you up. I'm tryna handle the shit without adding more bodies, so just… let me handle this, and y'all focus on keeping yo' nose clean. Aite?"

160

We both agreed and went back into the store. My mind was in overdrive as I thought about how I fucked up. I'd been doing this shit since I was fuckin' 15 years old. I didn't know how the fuck I slipped after all this time.

Fuck!

Chapter Eighteen

Karter

"That was sloppy, ladies! Do it again with energy this time! This is the first competition of this summer season, and I refuse to let y'all get out here and embarrass yourselves, me, AND your parents! Tori— start the music, please. It's not too late to get cut!" I yelled as the music started again.

I was a nervous wreck this past week, and I knew the girls probably thought I was losing my mind. Tomorrow, we were headed to Aurora, Illinois for the Around the World dance competition. If we won, or at least placed in the top three, we would be moving on to battle the winners in Indiana, and work our way around the world from there. I knew my girls could do it; they needed this touch love.

"Muuuch better! Those who are not in stands, you can go, but you better be at home practicing until you can do this routine in your sleep! Let you parents know to be here by 8 a.m. if you want to ride on the bus. We're pulling off at 8:30 on the dot, with or without you!"

For the rest of practice, I had Tori working the stand battle squad while I worked with Jayna and Tricee, who were doing the duo as well. These two were my strongest dancers, so I had full confidence in them.

"You all have to work on your stamina, and your breathing. You don't want to look tired while you're doing this. We need full energy. I want attitude, you need to slay!" They laughed, but I knew they were taking in what I said to them. Once it hit nine o'clock, like clockwork, Dez came to the studio and sat in my office until I was done, but I let the girls go shortly after so they could get some rest for tomorrow.

After that incident with Kevin, Dez had cameras installed in the parking lot, and there were more lights as well. He helped me into the passenger seat. The entire ride home was silent, as I guess we were both in our own thoughts, but Dez looked like the weight of the world was on his shoulders. When we made it home, he went right to the basement. I knew he went down there to smoke, so I didn't bother to follow him. Instead, I went to take a shower and get ready for bed.

When Dez finally came up to get in bed, it was one in the morning, and he smelled like he jumped in a bottle of Hennessy.

"Dez?" I turned over to look at him, and his eyes were closed.

"Hmm?"

"What's going on?"

"Life, baby. It's nothing for you to worry about, go to sleep." I chose not to push any further. For one, I was sleepy as hell and only had one eye open. And two, I guess he'd let me know when he was ready to share.

When my alarm went off at 6:30, Dez wasn't in the bed, and I didn't even know when he got up. I threw the covers back and got the bed so I could get ready. Once I handled all my business in the bathroom, I got dressed and went downstairs to look for Dez.

"Bae! Dezmund!"

silence

I called his phone, and he picked up on the second ring. "Wassup, baby?"

"Where are you? I didn't even know you left."

164

"I'm pulling up now, baby. I had to go take care of some shit. I didn't want to wake you up for that."

"Oh ok, well I'll see you when you get here." I hung up and went to the kitchen to pack my bag of snacks I needed for this ride. It was only about an hour and a half, but this baby had me hungry all the time. I heard honking outside and looked out the window. There was a big ass tour bus outside with Chicago Divas on the side of it. I ran outside, and my mouth was hanging down to the ground. Dez stepped out, and he was laughing at me.

"Close yo mouth, bae."

"What... how.... when..." I couldn't form a sentence as the waterworks started.

"Stop crying, bae. You ready to go?" He kissed me on the lips, and I nodded my head up and down. I grabbed my bag, camera, purse, and got on the bus. This was huge on the inside and looked luxurious as hell, like something those rappers be riding in when they're on tour.

Dez drove to the studio, and the parking lot was filled with cars. I was surprised everybody was early; usually, black people were on their own time. The girls were going crazy when they saw the bus, and they damn near knocked each other over to get on. Once the bus was packed and everyone was on, we got on the road, and my baby was doing flips the whole time. I guess he was as nervous as I was.

***

The ride back to the city was crazy. We won first place in the duo and stand category, and took second place for creative. Everyone was celebrating and took pictures with the trophies to post online.

"We gon' have to get you a big ass display case, bae. I know there's more to come," Dez said, rubbing my leg. He said he wasn't driving again, so one of the girl's dad agreed to drive back.

"I know, I'm happy as hell. I was so nervous, and yo' big head son ain't make it no better, doing karate all day."

"Ay, lil' dude, don't be hitting my wife, I don't discriminate." Dez was talking to my stomach and rubbing it, and the baby was kicking even more. He did this whenever Dez touched my stomach or talked to him. My baby knew his daddy's voice already. I couldn't wait until he got here. I just made 24 weeks, and was happy that I was more than halfway done with this pregnancy.

"You know you can't be doing that, he goes crazy when he hears you."

"That's my lil' homie, that's why." We pulled up to the studio, and everyone help unload the bus before they went on their way. I was going to have Mel plan something special for them. They worked hard, and I wanted to make sure they knew I see it.

"You wanna go grab something quick to eat?"

"After we parked this damn bus, yeah," I laughed and got comfortable in the passenger seat next to Dez.

"I'm proud of you, baby. I know you was nervous and shit, but I knew they was gon' kill. I mean, look at who their coach is."

"Aaww, don't gas me up, Dez."

When we got home, we switched cars and ended up at Louie's. They had the best steak, and I was craving one right now. We were seated right away in a private room that was in the back of the restaurant. I ordered us appetizers while we looked over the menu, and Dez had him a beer.

"What's on yo mind, Queen?"

"My mom has been asking for me to take her to Big Mama's grave, and I don't think I can do it. I can't even drive in that direction, let alone go stand over her." I shook my head and took a drink of my ice water. "I don't think I'm strong enough for that."

"I think it'll be good to go out there and put some new flowers down for her. When my pops died, I was the same way. I mean, he had split on us, then ended up dying and my mom wanted us to go show our respect and shit, but I wasn't feelin' it. Destini and Dame ended up going to the funeral, but I stayed my ass right the fuck home. It took me like a year to go see him, but I did it, and after I got everything off my chest, I felt better. I know it sound crazy, 'cause the nigga dead and I was just talkin' to a headstone. I knew he heard me, though." The waiter interrupted us when she brought our appetizer, and we put our food order in. I honestly didn't know what to say. I still don't think I was mentally or emotionally ready to go through that right now.

"I'll think about it."

"If you want, I'll go with you, baby; it ain't shit." Dez was smacking and stuffing these damn calamari in his mouth like it was the best thing since sliced bread, and I wanted to throw up.

"Thanks, bae." The rest of the dinner, we talked about baby stuff and decided that we were going to start getting his room together. I knew Dez wasn't gon' do nothing, but I always had Melodee for this.

Chapter Nineteen

Dezmund 'Dez'

Knock! Knock!

"Come in!"

"Dezmund Wright, you're a hard man to catch up to." I was handling paperwork for the club when Detective Normal walked in my office.

"I'm a busy man— how can I help you, Detective?"

"I still have this open case on my hands, and I was wondering if you can help me close it." Jazz's case was closed once me and Karter were cleared, but I knew she was talkin' about Karter's pops.

"I don't see how I could be of any assistance to you."

"Oohh, but you do. I don't know who you're protecting, or if you're just trying to save yourself, but I will find out."

"I'm sorry, I missed the question." Her white face was turning red, and I knew I was getting to her.

"I'm going to enjoy putting you away. You might have everyone else fooled, but I know exactly who you are, and what you're capable of. I'll see you soon, Mr. Wright."

She switched her flat ass out my office, and I blew out a deep breath. I swear, this bitch acted like she wanted some dick or something.

"Yo, what that bitch doing in here?" Dame came barging in my office and sat down on the couch, smoking a blunt.

"Gettin' on my damn nerves."

"I think that hoe tryna fuck or sumn'."

"I was just thinkin' that shit, bro." I laughed and the put the papers up that I was working on.

"What she say, though?"

"Same shit she always say. Y'all gon' be ready to move when it's time?"

"Hell yeah, I was born ready."

"Good."

"Let me run some shit by you, bro."

"Wassup?"

"I wanna marry Mel." I had taken a drink of water and ended up spitting the shit all over my desk when he said that. I knew this couldn't have been MY brother saying this. I had to be dreaming.

"Run that by me again?"

"I. Want. To. Marry. Melodee. Stop acting like that's so shocking."

"Shit, it is. Fuck you talkin' 'bout? What made you decide that, though, bro? That's a big step, it ain't shit to play about."

"Says the nigga that was proposing after the first day, fuck outta here."

"Touché, nigga. You ain't me, though. If you serious, though, you know Imma support it. You think she'll say yes?"

"She sho' the fuck better, she ain't got no choice." I shook my head at this nigga because he was dead ass serious.

"When you tryna do it?"

"After we get all this shit handled and can actually enjoy our fuckin' selves."

"You ain't never lyin', bro. A nigga feel like I aged a good 20 years over the last couple months, no lie." We stayed in my office talkin' for a while later, until I had to leave to meet Karter at the doctor's office. She was waiting for me inside, and she was deep in her phone when I walked in.

"Hey, baby. I thought you forgot." I kissed her and rubbed her protruding belly. Karter was literally all stomach, and if you saw her from behind, you wouldn't even know she was pregnant.

"Nah, I had to wrap shit up at the club." This appointment was quick as he just checked how big her stomach was, and told her the results of her blood test.

"Everything came back normal. You blood work did show that you are Rh negative, so I'm going to have my nurse come give you a shot of RhoGAM."

"What that mean? She ok? The baby ok?"

"Yes, they both are ok, but if she doesn't get this shot, her body can make antibodies that will look at the baby as something it has to fight off, and it'll be dangerous. This RhoGAM shot is given at 28 weeks, so she's right on time. Once the baby is born, you might have to get another one if they baby is RH positive, but don't panic. Everything is ok, I assure you."

Karter looked nervous, so I rubbed her thigh and she gave me a forced smile. "Thank you."

She left out, and the nurse came in a few minutes later with a big ass needle. Karter's ass cried like a damn baby when she got that shot in her ass. I literally had to hold her until she stopped.

"That shit hurt. If I gotta get that every time I get pregnant, this will be our one and only." I laughed, and she hit me in the chest hard as hell. Her heavy-handed ass be thinkin' I'm just being dramatic and shit, but nah, shit be hurtin'. I feel sorry for our kids when she has to whoop some ass.

I walked her to her car and opened the door for her. "I want to introduce our mothers, bae. They both need friends."

"It might be a good idea. Invite her over to Ma's Sunday."

"You sure? Shouldn't I call and ask if it's ok first?"

"I'll holla at her, don't trip." Her face lit up, and I kissed her again before I closed her door. I lived to see that smile on my wife's face; that's how I knew I was doing my job as a husband.

**

I dun gave the judge too many years,
years that I won't get baaaack!
And I swear I dun shed too many tears,
for niggas that I won't get baaack!

There was a party at the club tonight, so I came back to help Dame out since it was his turn to close. Kodak Black and PnB Rock's hit 'Too Many Years' was blaring through the speakers, and I nodding to the music. Destini came by with her new girl, and they ass was caked up in VIP section.

"Look at that nigga, Dez, rapping this shit like he did hard time or some shit," Destini yelled over the music, causing everybody to erupt in laughter.

"Fuck you, it felt like years in that muhfucka." I was babysitting my one cup of Hennessy since I was supposed to be in my business mode tonight. When the club closed at three, I was damn near throwing niggas out. By the time we left up outta there, it was a quarter to six and I was tired as hell.

Karter was asleep with my damn pillow between her legs, so I laid flat on the bed and was asleep in seconds.

"Dez! Wake up! Dez!"

"The fuuuuccccckkk." It felt like I had just closed my eyes when Karter was shaking my ass to wake up. "Wassup baby, you ok?" My eyes were closed, but I reached up and rubbed her stomach.

"No, it's a line of fuckin' squad cars at the gate." My eyes popped open, and I jumped out the bed. I checked the camera, and sure enough, there was that bitch, Normal, and five other fuckin' CPD cars lined up at my gate.

"It's cool, bae. Throw something on so I can see what they want." I threw on some sweat pants and slipped my foot in some Nike slides. Instead of opening the gate, I walked down to talk to them. "Well, good fuckin' morning, to what do I owe the pleasure?"

"I have a warrant to search the premises." She slid the warrant through the gate and snatched it.

Fuck!

I got my phone out my pocket and called Ivan. "Your wife already called, I'll be there in two minutes."

"Make it one." I hung up and hit the button to open the gate. I stood back, and Detective Normal walked in with a smug look on her face. "You mothafuckas bet not fuck my crib up, I know that much."

"What's going on, Dez?"

"Go wait at Dame's crib, bae. You don't need to be here." I said to Karter as she stood with her face balled up.

"No, I'm sitting here with you. What are they lookin' for?" We watched as they pulled the pillows out of the couch and threw them on the floor.

"A gun, Mrs. Wright, unless you want to help us out and tell us where the weapon is, and make everyone's job easier."

"I don't know what gun you're looking for, officer," Karter said smartly, and Detective Normal took a step closer to her.

"Yeah, aite. You better ask the last mothafuckin' pig that touched my wife, female or not."

"Are you threatening me?"

"It sounds like my client was just giving you some advice, Detective Normal. Good morning, everyone." Ivan walked in at the right time because I was about to break this bitch jaw about my mine.

"Got something!" One of the officers came from the basement with one of my guns, and Detective Normal was smiling like she just hit the lottery.

"Well, this looks like a match to my murder weapon. Which one of you does this lovely thing belong to?"

"It's mine," I spoke up and turned around to face Karter. "Call Dame and meet me down there. You already know where the cash at. Don't cry, Karter, you know I'll be good. I'll be back before lunch, Queen."

"Mr. Wright, can you step outside, please?" Detective Normal was smiling from ear and ear, and I just did what I was told. Ivan stood by me the whole time, and Karter was in the doorway on the phone with tears streaming down her beautiful face. "You have the right to remain silent. Anything you say can and will be used against you in a court of law." I was read my Miranda rights and put in the back of a fuckin' squad car…. again.

Chapter Twenty

Damien "Dame"

Boom! Boom! Boom!

Ding dong!

I opened my eyes and looked over at the clock. It was eight o'clock in the fuckin' morning, and somebody had the nerve to be banging on my damn door when I basically just went to sleep. I grabbed my 9mm from the nightstand and went downstairs. I snatched the door open, and Karter was standing there crying.

"You good? Where Dez at?" Seeing her breaking down like this had my heart beating fast as hell. I hope wasn't nothing wrong with my brother.

"He was arrested. They came and searched the house, and they took him! Y'all wasn't answering, and he told me to get you. Come on!"

"Fuck! Aite, let me go get Mel up." I took the stairs three at a time and rushed into the room.

"Mel! Wake yo ass up."

Smack!

I popped her ass and she jumped up in the bed, muggin' me. "What the hell I tell you about that shit, Damien?"

"Get up, Dez got arrested again. Karter downstairs flippin' the fuck out." She jumped up, grabbed something to throw on, and we were out the house in record time. Mel drove Karter's car, and I followed behind them. We pulled up to the precinct and rushed inside.

"I'm looking for my husband, Dezmund Wright, he was brought in." Karter was the first one at the desk, and the bitch behind it didn't look too pleased to be doing her fuckin' job.

"He's being processed right now. You folks can have a seat, and I'm sure his lawyer will update you soon."

Before I could snap, Melodee pulled me away, and we all sat waiting.

It seemed like hours went by before Ivan brought his short ass out to the lobby. "What the fuck is going on?"

"He's being charged with the murder of Kevin Martin. I was able to find a judge who's going to move his case first, so y'all can follow me down there."

I sent a text to Destini to let her know what was goin' on, and she said she was on her way. I knew she was goin' to say that, but it wasn't shit she could do here. I know her bean head ass wasn't gon' listen to me, so I didn't even try to talk her out of it.

***

"The court calls the case of The State of Illinois versus Dezmund Wright, case number 18 1 00098 8. Are you Dezmund Wright? Is that you correct name?"

"Yes, it is."

"You are being charged with the crime of first degree murder. This is a felony and holds a minimum sentence of 25 years. Do you understand the allegation against you, and the full range of punishment for this offense?" Dez nodded his head, and all you heard was

Karter next to me, and Melodee whispering to get her to calm down.

"How do you plead, guilty or not guilty?"

"Not guilty."

"I will accept your plea and enter it upon the docket of the Court. Bail will be set for $500,000, and if you can't make that, you will be held at Cook County Penitentiary until you can pay, or until you appear in court again." When the bail was set, Karter got up and ran out the courtroom. Mel followed her, and I waited until Dez was escorted out before I left.

Karter paid his bail, and it took these bitches another two fuckin' hours to let him go. He nodded for us to go outside, so we did.

"We gotta do this shit before I go back to court, this bitch playing games with me."

"I'm ready now, fuck," Destini's hot head ass spoke up first. People thought me and Dez were bad... nah, Dest had us beat, for real.

"And, if you do the shit, Imma be right the fuck back in jail. Let her think she can get comfortable, then we gon' hit."

We dapped each other up and went our separate ways. I rode home in thought, and Mel just had her hand on top of mine, but she didn't say a word. If I had to go confess to the shit I would, but my bro wasn't going back to jail. Then, these bitches talkin' 'bout first degree murder. They tryna bury my mans in there, and I ain't goin' for that fuck shit.

"Imma drop you off at home, I got a run to make."

"Dame, no— just come in with me and go back to sleep." I didn't bother answering as I continued to drive to the house. When we got to the house, and Melodee just sat in her seat and didn't move.

"Come on, Mel, just go in the house and I'll be back."

"No! Either bring yo ass in this house, or I'm going with you."

I laid my head on the headrest and had to count to twenty before I got out the car. I wanted to go make this bitch Normal suffer, but I saw I had to wait until Melodee's ass wasn't around.

"Why are you so mad, Damien? Do you wanna talk about it?"

"No, Melodee. Get the fuck out my face, man. I need some time! Damn, you get on my fuckin' nerves, bro."

"Fuck you and yo' ugly ass nerves! Have all the fuckin' time you need." She turned to leave out, and I grabbed her.

"Wait, I'm sorry."

"Yeah, you a sorry mothafucka! I don't know who the fuck you be thinkin' you talkin' to, Damien Marcellus Wright, but I will beat yo' damn head in!"

"Melodee, I said—"

"I don't give a fuck what you said! You got me fucked up!" She was pacing, lookin' crazy as hell, and I must be crazy too because this shit was turnin' me on.

"Melodee."

"What?!"

"I love you, I'm sorry." She squinted her eyes at me and sat on the couch. "I'm just… it's just… I can't explain the shit, man! If Dez ass get locked up for this shit, it ain't gon' be no lil' ass sixty days. That nigga said a MINIMUM of 25 years. He only fuckin' 30 years old, Mel! I'll lose my mind if I gotta go to a prison and talk to my brother through a glass."

"So, what were you going to do?"

"I ain't bringin' you in this shit," I said, shaking my head.

"Just tell me. What were you going to do?"

I thought about it for a minute before I answered. "Since she tryna take my brother from me, I was gon' take hers."

"Come back in one piece, and don't get caught." Melodee gave me a kiss and walked upstairs.

"Mel!"

"Yes?"

"Imma marry yo ass."

"I know, Damien— hurry up back."

"I'm serious, I love you."

"Love you too."

Chapter Twenty-One

Destini

"What this nigga look like?" Dame came and scooped me up and told me we were about to go have some fun. When he told me we were about get at the bitch Normal's brother, I got hyped as hell.

"There he go right there." I looked up to see a this little short, nerdy lookin' muhfucka walkin' down the street. We were in Steger, and it was dead as hell out here. I reached for the handle, and Dame stopped me. "Let him get settled first, then we going in."

I sat back, thinking of all the ways I could torture his ass, and I was getting hyped up. After thirty minutes, I was getting impatient, and I guess Dame noticed.

"Bring yo' ass on, man. You need to learn to control that shit."

"Fuck you, nigga." I grabbed my tool box from the back, and we walked up the street to his house and went to the back of the house. Dame picked the lock and slowly eased the door open. He screwed his silencer on his gun, and I stepped in behind, making sure to stay as quiet as I could. I heard the sound of a loud ass TV and followed it to the living room. "Ay!" I called out and watched as all the color drained from his face.

"Who… who are you, why are you in my house? You better leave before I call the cops."

"Like yo sister?" His eyes got big, and he started looking around.

Click!

The sound of Dame's gun cockin' had him pissin' on himself. "Take yo' pissy ass downstairs." He did as I said as he was begging for his life the whole time.

"Who are you? Why are you doing this? Is it money? I… I can get you money."

"Don't nobody want yo' money— sit in that chair over there, Jack."

"It's Henry."

"You getting smart with my sister, bitch?" Dame put his gun in his mouth, and he shook his head from side to side quickly. "Good, she said sit the fuck down, don't let her repeat herself."

Once he was in the chair, I tied him down and put a gag in his mouth. "You ain't got a weak stomach, do you bro?"

"I'm good, have your fun." I smiled and got my tool box, setting it on the table next to me. I pulled my first toy out, and his eyes got big. I grabbed my bayonet and stuck it in his side. He was trying to scream, but the gag in his mouth had it muffled.

"Did that hurt?" I laughed and snatched the knife out so I could stick it in the other side.

"Yo, Dest, yo ass startin' to scare me now. I'm ready to get the fuck outta here."

I kissed my lips and pulled my knife out of him. "Fine, do it the easy way then." I wiped my knife off and threw it back in my box.

Pew! Pew! Pew!

Dame sent three shots to his chest, and his body slumped over. "Scary ass nigga."

"Nah bro, you crazy as hell. I shouldn't have called yo' ass." I grabbed everything, and we left out the house.

The ride back to my house was quiet, and I was just smiling. I hadn't did that shit in so long, it felt good as fuck.

"You good?" Dame asked as he pulled up to my house.

"Yeah, nigga. I'll get at you." I dapped him up and went in the house. I turned my phone back on, and a text from Jakira popped up. I saw it was a meme, and I laughed loud as hell. We had been kickin' it regularly, and she was cool as hell. We just clicked, and she was goofy just like me, so we had hella fun together. My girl was definitely different, in a good way. She was my breath of fresh air.

Me: come over

Jakira: now?

Me: yeah, come on.

She responded saying she was on the way, so I took a hot ass shower to scrub any evidence off me and waited for her.

****

191

"Aaahhh, shiiiiit." Jakira came over and somehow, she ended up butt ass naked in my bed with me eating her pussy. Shit tasted like water, and I was having a field day on this shit. I think I was addicted already. I stuck a finger in her slippery tunnel, and she was shaking like she was having a seizure. I went back to eating her juicy peach, and I slurped up her juices as she came hard. As she laid in the bed, her chest was heaving up and down, I just laid down and got ready to go to sleep. I just wanted to see if she tasted as good as I thought, and she definitely did.

I think it was time she met moms, for real.

Chapter Twenty-Two

Dezmund "Dez"

Shit had been crazy since that whole raid shit went down, and Karter had been quiet the last couple of days. Whenever I asked her what was wrong, she would say *nothin'* and try to change the subject. I knew my baby was worried about me and thought I was gon' end up in jail, but that shit wasn't gon' happen. For one, I had those guns swapped already and two, I was handling that detective bitch once and for all tonight. Dame and Dest told me they murked her brother, and I saw the shit on the news. They ass didn't listen, but I wasn't mad 'cause they had to teach her a lesson. To us, family was everything and when you do something to harm one, then you got it from all of us.

I got eyes on her.

I got a text on my burner phone, and I already knew what it meant. It was time to end this shit finally.

"Baby?" I called out to Karter, who was busy reading on her Kindle.

"Yeah?"

"I gotta make a run, I'll be back in a few, aite?"

The look she was giving me was telling me that she wanted to pry and see where I was going, but she just nodded her head and said, "Ok, come back to me, please."

"Always, baby." I gave her a long, passionate kiss and smacked her on the ass before I left out. The whole ride on the other side of town, all I could think about was takin' my wife somewhere to clear her mind. The last thing I wanted her to do was to be stressing while she was carrying my seed. I pulled up on Detective Normal's block, and parked a few houses down from hers. I put my gloves on and walked coolly down the street, like I belonged there. I went to the car, where I had niggas sitting, and the window rolled down.

"Good lookin', y'all, you can go. Yo' money gon' be in yo' account."

"No problem, boss." They pulled off, and I walked up the stairs to her house. I rang the doorbell, and waited for her.

"That was fast how much— what the hell?" When she opened the door, I pushed in and closed the door behind me.

"Good evening, Detective Normal, how are you doing today?"

"How do you know where I live? You better get outta here; if you touch me, you will never see the light of day again." I let out a loud laugh, and leaned up against the wall.

"It's not hard for me to get some information. You know exactly who I am, remember? Have a seat, Heather." She moved slowly to the couch, and I took a pill bottle out of my pocket. "Here." I threw it to her, and she caught it and read the label.

"What is this? I'm not taking this, no." She threw it on the table, so I took the gun from the back of me.

"You're either gonna die painless, or I'm going to call my sister and let her dig your fuckin' eyeballs out, then I'm going to shoot you. But, understand this, whether you choose or I do, you're dying tonight."

She was crying, making the ugliest face, and I checked my watch to show her how uninterested I was in those tears. "Are you done? I don't have all night, my wife is waiting on me."

"I. I'm not taking those."

"And THIS is why I said you are a pain in my ass." I swiftly walked to her and grabbed her face with one hand. She tried to fight, so I stuck my gun in her mouth. "I see I have to make the decision for you."

"No, no, no, ok, I'll take the pills, just please!"

"That sounds better." I popped the top open and handed her four pills. The guy I got 'em from said I only needed two, but I wanted to make sure this bitch was gone and outta my hair.

"Can I at least have water?"

"Bitch, use yo' spit!" She wanted to play, and I was three seconds away from filling her up with lead. She took the pills, and I stood there until I saw the life leave her eyes, then I left out the same way I came. When I got far enough away from her house, I turned my phone on and had what seemed like a hundred damn text notifications. One caught my eye, and I started to panic as I sped down I-94 West.

Dez, come to the hospital now! It's Karter!

****

"Where is she? What happened?" I ran through Christ hospital like a fuckin' tornado, lookin' for my wife.

"Sir, you have to relax and tell me who you're looking for."

"Karter. Karter Wright, where is she?"

"Third floor. Sir you need a pass!" I kept going and got on the elevators. I hoped my baby was ok. Shit, both of 'em. I was taken to Karter's room, and she was laid in the bed with her back to the door.

My heart dropped as walked closer to the bed. "Kay? Is it the baby? Is the baby ok?"

"He's ok, he just tried to make his appearance early."

"I know it's my fault you stressin' and shit, but I promise, it's over now baby."

"Dez, it's not your fault, calm down." She had my face in her hands, and we just stared into each other's eyes. I think I fell in love with my wife all over again.

"Can you travel?"

"I don't think so, I'll be on bed rest." I climbed in the little ass hospital bed with her, and she fell asleep in my arms. I was uncomfortable as hell, but like I said before, I'd do anything for my wife.

Chapter Twenty-Three

Melodee

"Come on, Karter. You gotta have a baby shower, you been in this damn bed for yearrrsssss. Probably got bed sores and shit." She threw a pillow at me, and I ducked. Dez asked me to convince Karter to change her mind about a baby shower, and she was being stubborn as hell. Ever since she had that scare a few weeks ago, she's really been scared to get out the bed. I came over the other day, and she had Dez carrying her ass to the bathroom. This shit was outta control.

"Whhyyyy, I don't want to overdo it and have something happen. Everything has been perfect since I been on bedrest, and I'm just scared."

"What if we have it here? I could get it set up in that big ass yard, and you can sit in the damn chair all day."

She sighed heavily, and I was trying not to smile because I knew I had her. "Fine, you can go ahead and do it."

"Me and my godson thank you."

"You and your godson is irra. How's everything going so far with the business and stuff, though?"

"It's been moving, you know. I'm still tryna get my name out there, but it's good."

"I'm so proud of you, Melly Mel."

"Don't you get all emotional and shit, Karter. Oh my God, what you crying for?" She shrugged her shoulders and tried to wipe her tears away. "Remind me to neeeeeever get pregnant if it's gon' do me like that."

"I can't help it, it's these damn hormones. One minute I'm happy, then I'm crying, then I'm pissed and ready to fight. I've been dealing with this for six and a half months, but I know once DJ gets here, it'll be all worth it."

"Eeewww, you naming my baby after that scrub?" I laughed and the next thing I knew, I was on the floor. I looked up, and Dez was standing behind me laughing.

"Watch ya mouth, Mel."

"Imma kick yo' ass if you push me like that again. I don't care how big you is," I said, getting off the floor and making sure he ain't scrape my damn knee. Ain't nothing worse than some black ass kneecaps

"I ain't Dame, I'll flex yo' lil' ass in here."

"Yeah, and you better ask Dame about me. I fight dirty. You gon' fuck around and lose an eye messing with me."

"Okaaaayy, you damn fools," Karter interrupted us.

"That's yo' husband, bro. I gotta get outta here anyway, got a consultation with a potential client. Dez, the baby shower is on, so I'll be sending you the bill, homie." Dez walked me outside, and I hopped in Dame's Range Rover Sport. I needed a truck, especially for the days I had an event. Maybe I could talk Dame into letting me have this one.

I drove to the loft office space I was renting on Randolph, and I was praying it wasn't any traffic on the expressway. I made it there in record time and parked right in front. I could've put it in the garage, but Dame would've had a fit.

"Good morning, Ms. Barnett, your messages are on your desk," my assistant spoke as soon as I walked in.

"Good morning, and thank you, Lisa." I walked in my office, and there were flowers all over my desk. I looked at the card, and it was from Dame. My baby had been stepping his romance game up… must've got some pointers from Dez, 'cause lawd knows Damien didn't think of this himself.

"Ms. Barnett, your 11 o'clock is here."

"Send them back, thank you." I stood up and straightened my blouse and pencil skirt. I plastered on the best smile I could, and it was wiped away when I saw my mother walk in the door.

"I can guess from the scowl on your face that you're not too happy to see yo' mother, Melodee dear."

"You don't have to guess, I'm not happy to see you. But please, have a seat." I pulled out my legal pad so I could jot down notes.

"So, where are the owners? I would love to compliment them on the décor in here."

"I am the damn owner, now let's get down to the detail of this event. Who or what is it for? Is there a theme, or a budget?"

"Well, your father is retiring, and I want to give him the most extravagant retirement party ever." I stared at my mother, and she still looked the same since the last time I saw her almost eight years ago. The fact that she was being so nonchalant like she hadn't seen her daughter in almost a decade was blowing me, but I sucked it up, kept my personal feelings at bay, and wrote down her requests.

"Ok, so when do you want this done? Do you have an estimate on guests?"

"Roughly around 150 people, give or take a few, and I need to have this done before the end of the month. That's not a problem, is it dear?" I looked at the calendar, and it was the fuckin' 16th. I didn't know if this heffa was tryna test me, but she didn't know I was all about a challenge.

"Of course not."

"Great, I'll be in touch, do you have a personal number?"

"Nope, business phone works just fine. Lisa will get your guest list and deposit from you at the front, and we'll be in touch." I shook her hand and forced a smile on my face. By the time she left out, my cheeks were hurting, and I wanted a drink and four blunts.

Since I didn't have a lot of time to get everything together, I got started calling around for venues and caterers. She wanted an *extravagant* retirement party, so that's what she was gon' get.

I worked straight through my lunch break and by time I left the office, my stomach was sucking on my back. While I drove home, I called Dame to see if he ate already.

"'Bout time yo' bald head ass called me."

"Don't answer the phone like that. Did you eat already, because I'm fuckin' starvingggg?"

"What you want to eat?"

"Cat and wing dinner from Harold's."

"Aite, you on yo' way to the crib?"

"Yes, please let it be there waiting for me, or Imma die." I hung up and sat in the damn downtown traffic. I was probably better off hopping on the damn redline.

It took me 45 minutes to get home, and Dame was standing at the front door holding my food for me. "Thank you so much, baby. I didn't even stop to take a lunch today." I sat at the table, and Dame sat across from me with his food.

"Why not? Don't do that shit no mo', you know you been crazier than usual when you hungry." I laughed, but he was right. I got hangry (hungry and angry) if I didn't eat.

"My mother came by, wanting me to plan my father's retirement party. I wanted to send that bitch right back out the door, but I ain't turnin' down no money."

"Yeah, you gotta shit on 'em one time for the fun time, love."

We ate our food, and I laid on Dame's lap as he played the game. This was a good chill night for us, and I liked just sitting in the house sometimes. After working at the club and going through my turn-up phase, I actually didn't get excited about going out anymore. I was turning into an old lady. Dame's phone rang, and he tapped me so he could get it out his pocket.

"Let me go take this." He stood up and walked outside to answer his phone. *Dame got me fucked up.*

Chapter Twenty-Four

Damien "Dame"

"Hello?"

"Hi, Mr. Wright. Your piece is done; when do you want to come pick it up?"

"I can get it tomorrow sometime. When do you open?"

"We're open at nine am, sir."

"Ok, I'll be there." I hung up and turned around to see Melodee standing in the doorway with her arms folded across her chest.

"When you start going outside to talk on the phone?" Her eyes squinted at me as I walked closer to her. When I was within arms reach, I grabbed her and mushed my lips into hers.

"It was something confidential, baby. You'll know soon, just trust yo' man."

"Ok, let you be on some bullshit, and Imma dot yo' damn eye." She tried walked off, and I smacked her on the ass.

"You know that shit turn me on, baby. Come take care of daddy."

"I need a shower, move."

"Well, I'm coming too, shit." I followed her to the bathroom and she was sitting there laughing and smiling, like I was playing or something, but I stripped out of my clothes and got in with her.

At first, I just stood back and admired Melodee's perfectly round ass as the water cascaded down her back. She had some stretch marks back there, but that shit was sexy as hell to me. Melodee looked back at me, and my heart felt like it was beating out of my chest.

"Get over here." My voice was low, but she heard me clearly. Biting her lip, she walked over the where I was and dropped to her knees. I ain't even want no head, but I wasn't turning the shit down.

"Fuuuucckk." She took me in her mouth, and I almost lost it when I felt the back of her throat. I was tryna keep my hands to myself, 'cause Mel hated when I grabbed her head and shit, but I couldn't help it. I felt my nut rising and tried to move her, but she kept going until my kids were shooting down her throat. She kept suckin', knowing how sensitive I was, so I grabbed a handful of her hair.

She stood up licking her lips, and I was right back standing at attention. "Imma get you back for that one," I said as I lifted her up and entered her slowly. Her legs were wrapped around my waist as I moved her up and down on my pole.

"Uuugghhh." She groaned into my ear as I pushed my dick all the way inside her moist tunnel. The only sound you heard was our skin slapping, and moaning. I pulled out of her and put her on her feet.

"Turn around and grab them ankles." She did what I said, and I didn't show no mercy on her pussy. She tried to stand up, and I slapped her ass.

Whap!

"Grab them ankles. I ain't tell you to move, did I? Did daddy tell you to get up, Mel?"

"Aaahhh, noooo."

"Throw that ass back, Mel. Yeah, just like that, shiiiiit." I sped my pace up and came so hard, I pushed Mel and she almost fell.

"If I would've broke my damn neck in here because of yo' ass..." We shared a laugh, washed up, and went to the room to get dressed. I watched Mel move around the room doing her nightly routine, and I wanted to ask her right now if she wanted to marry me. I'd be damned if I asked her in front of muhfuckas and she said no or some shit.

"Melodee."

"Hmmm?"

"You love me?"

"Yeah, I love you."

"Like... how much?"

She stopped twisting her hair to turn around and look at me. "What the hell did you do, Damien?"

"Just answer the question."

"I love you enough to kill you if you about to say you cheated on me."

"You know ain't nobody cheat on you girl, damn."

"Ok, just checking." Instead of pressing the issue, I let it go and waited for her to get in the bed. I just knew if she said anything but yes, she was gon' catch these hands. Dead ass serious.

****

"Damn bro, you was for real about this, huh?" Dez asked as I examined the five-carat, cushion-cut diamond ring I was going to propose to Melodee with.

"Yeah, I was for real. That's my baby, and I want her to know that I want this shit forever."

"My son growin' up, mane." He put his hand on my shoulder, and I shrugged it off.

"Fuck outta here, yo' ass got one son and that nigga still baking."

"Aite, when Karter beat yo' ass bout callin' him a nigga, you gon' learn."

"Nigga, you the only one scared of her." I handed the ring back to the jeweler so she could pack it up, and somebody caught my attention. It looked like Melodee's bitch ass ex, but I wanted to be sure before I knocked the wrong nigga out.

"Here you are, sir, and good luck."

"Thanks." I snatched the bag and left out the store. I went in the direction I saw that nigga walk off to, and Dez was right next to me.

"Fuck you goin'? I ain't say I was shoppin' with yo' ass, I got shit to do today."

"Shut the fuck up. If this that nigga Rodney, I'm 'bout to piece his ass up real quick, then we can go."

"Come on, bro, let it go. Whatever happened, happened. Let's get the fuck outta here. I ain't tryna see no more fuckin' police or jail cells." I listened to what he was saying and decided to leave, like he said. Don't get it twisted, though; when I caught this nigga somewhere secluded, it was a wrap.

Chapter Twenty-Five

Destini

"Yo Dest, I need a ride to the crib. Jakira ass ain't answering the phone. You heard from her?" Kolby asked, barging into my office.

"Ay, lil' nigga, you cool and all, but Imma need you to knock next time," I said as I finished up this payroll shit I had to do.

"My bad, bro."

"And naw, I ain't heard from her, but I need a minute and we can go." It was after nine at night and the store was closed, but I still had paperwork to finish.

"Aite, ain't like I'm goin' nowhere." He sat at the couch in my office, and I went back to finishing up.

When I was done, I grabbed all my shit and we left after making sure everything was locked up. I had Kolby roll up while I drove, and we smoked and vibed to music while I drove toward his crib.

"The fuck truck is that?" Kolby spoke aloud as we pulled up to the house. Not thinking nothing of it, I parked and waited for him to get out.

"Yo' ass need to buy a damn whip, bro. Matter fact, I'll give you one of mine. I'm tired of chauffeuring yo' bean head ass around."

"Man, all my money go to my daughter and shit." Their front door opened, and some big ass nigga walked out with Jakira right behind him, wearing a long ass shirt, and I saw her ass poking out the bottom of it.

"The fuck?" Before I knew it, I was out the car and making my way over to them. She was so busy smiling all in his face that she didn't even see me approaching.

"I'll hit you up later, baby."

"Dest!" She was looking like a deer caught in headlights, and everything in my head was telling me to light both of they asses up.

"Fuck is going on?"

"Nothing. He... he was just—"

"Fuckin' yo' rat ass? Yeah, I can see that." I shook my head and walked back to my car. If she wasn't my homie's sister, this bitch would be pickin' up her teeth off the porch.

"Destini! Wait! Let me explain." Jakira was running up to my car and in my head, I was thinking if she knew what God loved, she'd stay out the street.

I sped off and headed to Ma's house. I knew she was asleep, but I needed her right now. My mama was my best friend, and she was the one person, besides my brothers, who knew how to calm me down when I was ready to do something crazy.

Surprisingly, the lights inside were on, so I parked and used my key to let myself in. I walked through the house, until I found her in the kitchen making cakes and shit.

"Ma, why you up baking this late?" I asked as I walked around the counter and gave her a kiss on the cheek, then sat at the island.

"Dest, what are you doing here, baby?" Before I could answer her, my ringing phone interrupted me. I saw it was Jakira calling, and I slammed it face down on the counter. When I looked back up at Ma, she must've saw the fire in my eyes because she stopped what she was doing and sat down next to me. She grabbed my hand, and I lowered my head. "Father God, I come to you with my baby, asking to remove all those evil thoughts out of her mind, Lord. Keep leading her on the right path of greatness, Father." My mama prayed for me, and I felt the pressure lifting off my shoulders. She used to pray over me all the time when I was younger and tell me that she could tell I was fighting a battle no one else knew about, and she was right. It wasn't even about me being lesbian, and even though she didn't agree with my lifestyle, she accepted me and always told me how much she loved me. It was the fact that I enjoyed torturing people. To see the amount of pain I could inflict on a person made me wet.

"Amen."

"Amen." I zoned out and didn't even hear the rest of the prayer. I did feel better, though.

"You might as well stay, you don't need to be out driving anymore."

I agreed and went to my old room so I could shower and lay down. I heard my phone going off, but I already knew who it is was, and I'd deal with that shit when I was in a better head space.

The next day, I went home and saw Jakira sitting on my porch. I started to keep going, but I parked and got out. "Can we talk?"

"For what?"

"I'm sorry."

silence

"Can you say something?"

"I ain't got shit to say. Is that all, though? I got shit to do."

"So, that's just it? We're done?"

"Hell yeah, I don't give second chances, fuck outta here. Tell Kolby come grab his whip later, though." I walked around her and went in the house. Ma would be proud of me; I kept my hands to myself.

Kolby stopped by later in the day to pick a car, and I let him have my candy red Camaro. He tried to talk to me for his hoe ass sister, but I waved that shit off. I was definitely the wrong muhfucka to ask for seconds chances from. Better take her ass to church if she was looking for forgiveness.

Kolby told me he was finally getting his daughter back, so I gave him a week off of work to handle daycare and whatever else he needed for her. We smoked a few blunts before he left, and I finished chillin' in the crib alone. I think I liked it this way.

Chapter Twenty-Six

Melodee

It was finally the day of this damn retirement party, and I was nervous as hell. Thankfully, Dame agreed to come with me, so I didn't have to deal with them by myself.

"Damn, you looking sexy as fuck, bae. Can I get a quickie in before we go?" Dame came up behind me while I was looking in the full-length mirror, and I pushed him away from me.

"No! And you better move." I gave myself another once-over, and I had to toot my own horn. I was wearing a strapless, navy blue dress that stopped at the middle of my thigh, and I paired it with my favorite pair of navy and silver Jimmy Choo pumps.

"That's cool, I'll rip that shit off later."

"No the hell you won't, not with how much I paid for this dress." I turned around to examine Dame and had to lick my lips because bae was lookin' real Zaddy-ish. He had just got a fresh cut, and his thick beard was shining from the coconut oil he put in it. He was matching me, wearing a navy blue Tom Ford suit I pick out for him, and he had on some loafers to match.

"You ready to go see what these old fuckas talkin' bout, Mel?" I laughed and grabbed my clutch off the dresser.

"Yeah, come on." We walked out the house, and I stood there frozen in place staring at this all black Rolls Royce Ghost that was parked in the driveway.

"Pick ya lip up, baby. I told you, you gotta shit on 'em one time. Show 'em you making major moves without that piece of fuckin' paper.

I was smiling like a kid in a candy store as I walked down the steps with Dame behind me. The driver got out and tried to open the door for me, but Dame stopped him.

"Nah, I got this, bro. Gon' head and get back in the car."

I apologized to the guy with my eyes and hit Dame in his chest. "Stop Damien. He's just doing his job, I'm sure."

"His job is to drive this muhfucka. I got my girl's door and shit." I shook my head and climbed in the back. I was loving the inside, and I was thinking about checking my piggy bank so I could get me one of these bad boys.

My stomach was doing flips the closer we got to the venue, and Dame must've sensed my uneasiness because he kept rubbing my thigh. "Calm down, you know I got yo' back." I blew out a deep breath as the car came to a halt, and Dame helped me out of the car.

It was still an hour and a half before the guests were supposed to arrive, so I just double and triple checked everything, and it was perfect. I knew my parents and their bourgeois ass friends were gonna like this.

Like clockwork, at eight on the dot, the guests start arriving and I greeted everyone that came in, until Lisa needed my help with something. I left Dame to mingle with people as I handled my business.

***

"Ahh there you are, Melodee dear. Are you going to come speak to your father?" I'd been avoiding them all night, but like the bloodhound she is, my mother sniffed me out of the crowd.

"Sure, I'll find you all in a minute."

"Why wait? Come on, your little friend can come too," she said, referring to Dame.

"Bi—"

"I said, I'll find him in a minute. I have to go check on the food." I knew Dame was getting ready to cuss her the fuck out, and I wanted to get through this party without any hiccups. I pulled Dame to the kitchen with me, and he had a mug on his face.

"Yo, she got me fucked up talkin' 'bout your *little* friend. Better tell her ain't shit little over here, g," he seethed and grabbed an appetizer off the tray, and stuck it in his mouth. He spit it right back out in his hand, and I was bent over laughing at the disgusted look on his face. "That taste like some shit cake, fuck is that?"

"That's what you get for touching stuff. You good now? Because I'm ready to get this shit over with." He nodded and we walked out the kitchen, hand in hand. We walked to where my parents were and immediately, all eyes were on us.

"Well, isn't this a surprise. When your mother told me you were here, I didn't believe her. You look… hmmm. That dress is a bit much for the occasion, don't you think?"

"Naw, my girl look good as fuck, if you ask me." Dame interrupted him and stepped in front of me.

"And, who are you supposed to be?" he asked with his nose turned up.

"I'm gon' be the one to knock you the fuck out if you say somethin' else outta pocket 'bout my girl." This little chat was going left quick, and I knew Dame wasn't going to back down, especially since my mother already pissed him off.

"I'm not surprised this is who you're with, Melodee. You always had a thing for these—" My father wasn't able to finish his sentence before Dame punched him in the mouth.

My mouth was hanging open in an O, and my mother was screaming like somebody hit her ass too. "You two need to leave!" She screamed as she checked on my father, who was asleep on the floor.

"Proudly, make sure you give my assistant that other half of that check before you leave." I grabbed Dame and power-walked out the door. I know somebody probably called the police, and I was gon' be knocking my mother's ass out too if Dame got arrested.

Thankfully, the driver was still sitting outside, so we ran across the lot to the car and jumped in. He pulled off, and I looked over at Dame before we both erupted in laughter. "I can't believe you did that," I said in between breaths.

"Man, Moms better be lucky I don't hit women, because she was about to catch the left one to her chin." I couldn't breathe from how hard I was laughing at him. "Ay, my man, make a right up here, I'm hungry as hell." The driver did what he was told, and we pulled up in front of Petterino's. It was an Italian restaurant, and I heard they had pretty good food. They were expensive as hell, so I'd never been; shit was too rich for my blood.

"You tryna come grab sumn 'to eat, bro?" Dame spoke to the driver.

"No sir, I'm fine."

"Aite, suit yourself, we'll be back." He got out and helped me out as well. Dame slid the host a hundred-dollar bill, and we were taken to a table right away. Looking at the menu, I was ready to say fuck this and go home to cook. Who the hell was paying $48 for some damn steak? That shit musta been coated in gold.

"Welcome to Petterino's, can I start you all off with some drinks?"

"Yeah, let us get a bottle of yo' best wine, my man. By time you come back, we should be ready." The waiter walked away, and I continued to look over the menu.

"What you getting?" I asked, not being able to decide what I wanted.

"Imma try this salmon shit."

"I think I want chicken, I don't even know what the hell half of this says."

"Shit, me either. We should've grabbed some pizza or something." I agreed, and we shared a laugh as we continued to scan the menu.

The waiter came back with our bottle, and we placed our order and waited for him to come back. Dame poured our glass, and he took his to the head like it was a cup of Kool Aid and refilled it.

"Slow down before you be drunk as hell in here," I said as I brought my glass to my mouth and sipped.

"I gotta piss, I'll be back." I shook my head at him and took another sip of my wine. It took him almost five minutes to come back, and he was sweating like somebody was chasing him.

"You good?"

"Hell naw."

"What's wrong? What happened that fast?" Dame stood up and walked around the table. When he got down on one knee next to me, my heart dropped to my stomach and my mouth was in my lap. There were gasps, and people cheering as Dame pulled a red velvet box out of his pocket.

"I been carrying this shit around for a minute, just trying to find the best way to ask you. You know I ain't good at this type of shit, Mel, but..." He opened the box, and my eyes were big staring at the ring that was in it. "Will you marry a nigga?"

I laughed at his ghetto ass proposal and held my hand out. "Yes, Dame, I'll marry a nigga."

"For real?" He looked shocked that I actually said yeah, and I nodded my head yes. He slipped the ring on my finger, and this bitch was shining. I pulled his face to mine and planted a deep kiss on his lips. There were cheers all around us, and I was smiling from ear to ear. Dame got up as the waiter came back with our food, and he asked him to bring the check and some to-go boxes.

"I'm ready to go home and fuck the shit outta my fiancée, hurry up."

After he paid, we grabbed our food and left out so we could go home. We made love all night to celebrate our engagement, and even though I never thought I'd be getting married, I was excited to marry my best friend.

The next morning, we sent out texts telling our family we were getting married, and everyone was as excited as we were. I couldn't wait until our wedding. I knew it was gon' be lit.

Chapter Twenty-Seven

Karter

"You want me to go with you?"

"No, I need to do this alone." I finally agreed to take my mom to the cemetery to see Big Mama, and today, on her birthday, I was finally going to do it.

"Call me if you need me, baby." I grabbed my purse off the couch and gave Dez a kiss before I left. When I pulled up to my mom's house, I honked and she came right out.

"Hey sweetie, how are you feeling?" she said when she climbed into the passenger seat.

"I'm doing good, how are you?"

"I've been good, going stir crazy in the house alone. I crocheted a lot of hats and booties for the baby." Her face lit up when she talked about my son, and it warmed my heart.

"Do you have a license? There's a car in the garage. I don't know where you're going to go, but at least you'll have the option."

"Yeah, I have my license but like you said, I have nowhere to go."

"Dez's mom don't live too far. Maybe I'll introduce you all. She has Sunday dinner at her house every week. If you want, I'll make sure it's ok, but you could tag along too."

"Oh, that sounds great. It'll be nice to finally have a friend."

We arrived at Burr Oak cemetery, and my heart was beating out of my chest. "Are you ok, Karter?"

"Yeah, come on." I grabbed the flowers I picked up and my blanket from the backseat before I got out of the car. The closer we got to Big Mama's plot, the harder it was for me to breathe. When I saw the headstone with her picture, I broke down crying like she had just died. I laid my blanket in the grass and sat down. My mother sat down on the other side, with her own tears running down her cheeks. Silently, we cleaned around her headstone and put the fresh flowers down.

"Hey, Mommy. I'm sorry it took me so long to come see you. I hope you know I thought about you every day, Ma. I wish I would've come to see you sooner. I know it would've have saved you, but at least I could've said bye." I sat listening to my mom pour her heart out, and it was hard for me to control my emotions. When she was done, she kissed Big Mama's picture and walked back to my car. I sat there for a few moments, just staring down at the grass. After ten minutes, my mom came to help me up off the ground and walked me back to the car. I got in the passenger side, and she drove us back to her house. I was quiet the whole ride back, and she was too.

"Do you want to come in for a minute?"

"Yeah, I could do that." We got inside, and the house was spotless.

"You want something to drink?"

"A bottle of water is fine." I got comfortable on the couch, and she walked to the kitchen. My phone vibrated, and I pulled it out and saw a text from Dez.

Dez: Everything ok?

Me: yeah, back at her house, I'll be home soon.

Dez: take your time, baby, I was just checking on you

*Me: thanks baby, love you *kiss emoji**

Dez: love you more

"Here you go." My mom handed me the bottle of water and sat down next to me.

"We haven't really had time to talk, but I just wanted to see how you felt about me being there for the baby? I know you probably won't trust me right away to be alone with him, but I want to at least be there when he's born, if that's ok."

"I don't have a problem with you being in your grandson's life."

"Thank you so much. Do you mind if I ask you something?"

"Go ahead." I turned to face her, and she was playing with the ring on her hand.

"Did Dez…. did he kill Kevin?" I stared at her blankly for about ten seconds before I stood up.

"That's my cue to leave." Dez was cleared of all charges, but I didn't like her asking questions, especially when I put all of that behind me already.

"Wait, I didn't mean to upset you, I'm sorry."

"The keys to the car are in the lock box, and the code is 0906. See you tomorrow." I walked out and got in my car to leave. I called Melodee, and she answered on the first ring.

"Hey, boo."

"What you doing? I feel like you been abandoning me?"

"Karter, I just talked to you last night."

"But, when's the last time you *saw* me?"

"You coming to Ma's tomorrow?"

"Yeah, I'll be there."

"Well, there ya go. I'll see you then." I kissed my teeth, and Melodee laughed.

"I'm just playing, you big baby. I can stop by today, if you want."

"Yes, I need you, bf."

"What's wrong? I gotta come kick Dez's ass?" This was why I loved Mel. My best friend was ready for whatever. Even if she knew she wasn't gon' win, she was still coming ready.

"No, fool. I just went to see Big Mama, and I need one of my best friend nights."

"Enough said, I'll bring the ice cream and shit." I agreed, and we got off the phone when I pulled up to the house. Dez came outside when I pulled in the gate and opened my door for me.

"You must've missed me or something."

"I always miss you when I ain't with you, baby." He helped me out and closed the door.

"So, how did everything go?"

"It was hard, but I'm glad I finally went. I cried like a baby, but I needed that."

"Was it awkward with your mom there?" I got comfortable on the couch, and Dez put my feet in his lap to rub them.

"Not really, the whole visit was actually nice. I wanted to ask Ma is it ok if she comes tomorrow."

"I'm sure she won't mind."

"She did ask something that had me side-eyeing her?"

"Which was?"

"If you killed Kevin." His jaw flinched, and he ran his hand down his goatee.

"And, what you say?"

"Shit, nothing. I told her ass that was my cue to leave, and I did."

"Well, don't worry about that, baby. That shit is over and behind us now. The only thing we got to worry about is our baby staying inside until it's time to pop up outta that thang."

We stayed on the couch watching TV, until Melodee showed up with Dame and our girls' night turned into card night. They were drinking while I had to sit my pregnant ass there sober with my apple juice.

"When y'all tryna get married?" I asked Dame and Melodee. They both looked at each other and shrugged.

"We ain't decided on a date yet. I know I'm tryna have a destination wedding. I'm tryna go fuck up another country and bring my ass home."

"That should be fun. I'm so happy for y'all."

"Aaww shit, Karter about to start crying. Come on, Mel," Dame said, causing everybody to laugh, and I stuck my middle finger up at him. These two are like the perfect couple; they both played too damn much.

When Melodee got drunk, they left and we got ready for bed.

The next morning, we got up, got dressed, and I sent my mom a text where to meet us. Ma said weeks ago that she could've came over, but I wanted to make sure she wasn't on bullshit.

"You ok over there, Karter baby?"

"Yeah Ma, I'm fine." We were all at Ma's house, and thankfully, her and my mother were getting along well.

"You sure? You looking uncomfortable." When she said that, Dez paused the game he was playing and Dame and walked over to me.

"I'm fine, Dez, stop." He looked at me like he didn't believe me and sat next to me, rubbing my stomach. I flinched a little because my stomach was tight, and it was painful when he touched it.

"How long you been having that pain, Karter?" He asked with a stern look on his face. I put my head down, and he lifted it back up so I was looking in his eyes.

"It started this morning, but I'm fine, Dez. Really."

"Bring yo ass on, Karter!" I jumped when he raised his voice, and his face softened when he saw the tears building up in my eyes. "Look, I'm sorry, but you know you can't keep stuff like this away from me."

"I know," I said lowly, and stood up so we could leave.

"I'll call y'all when we know something."

We got in the car, and the ride was quiet... like awkward as hell quiet. I wasn't used to this type of vibe with us, but I guess that was my fault for holding this in. I really didn't think it was anything serious because I'd been feeling him move around, so I knew he was ok, right?

Dez pulled up to Christ Hospital, and he still hadn't said a word to me. "I'll go get a wheelchair, hold on." Well, that was the only thing he said to me in the last twenty minutes.

He got out the car and came back seconds later with a nurse and a wheelchair. They rolled me in, and Dez went to park his car. I was immediately taken up to the labor and delivery floor, and hooked up to all the machines. When Dez came in my room, he pulled a chair up to the bed and just stared off into space.

"Are you mad at me, Dezzy?" I poked my lip out in a pout, and he just shook his head.

"Don't do that Dezzy shit, man. Yeah, I'm mad."

Knock! Knock!

"Hello, I'm Georgia, and I'll be your nurse. What brings you in today?"

"My wife is hardheaded, and she been in pain all day." I rolled my eyes at his pettiness, and the nurse laughed.

"What type of pain, is it like contractions? Or discomfort?"

"A little of both," I admitted, and avoided Dez's eyes.

"Ok, lay back and I'll check you. I see on the monitors that you've been having a few contractions, and baby is not liking it. How far along are you?"

"I just made 34 weeks." Dez moved out of the way while the nurse checked me. The feel of her hands was painful, and I wanted to kick her in the damn face.

"Ok, you look to be at three, maybe three and a half centimeters. I'll be right back with the doctor." The look on her face read that it was more than what she was telling me, and I started to panic, but she ran out the door before I could ask any questions.

I silently cried, and Dez came back to my bedside to wipe my tears. "Just relax. Everything is ok, my boy is strong, and both of you are going to be fine, you hear me?" I just nodded my head, and he wiped the fresh tears that had fallen.

The nurse came back with the doctor, and he was pushing an ultrasound machine. "Hello, I'm Dr. Perez. I'm the on-call physician today, and I'm just going to get a quick peek at baby, ok?"

"Yes, that's fine."

He sat in a rolling chair and squeezed some gel onto my stomach. He kept the screen turned away from me, and I wanted to see what he was looking at. "Ok, mom and dad, it looks like baby's going to be making an early arrival, but he's breech and is not responding well to the contractions. So, I want to get in there and get him out ASAP."

"It's… it's too early."

"Yes, it is a bit early, but you don't want him to stay in there. At 34 weeks, he has a great chance of survival, and we have a great team here to care for you and baby." I looked over at Dez, and worry was written all over his face. I felt like a terrible mom already; I couldn't even protect my baby while he was inside of me. The doctor walked out the room, and I missed the ending of whatever he just said.

"Bugs, don't cry. It's ok, they said he's going to be ok." Dez tried to make me feel better, but I could tell he didn't even believe what he was saying.

"Can you go let everyone know what's going on, please?"

"Yeah, Queen. I'll be right back." Dez kissed me on my forehead before he walked out the room. The second the door closed, I was crying and praying that my baby made it out of this okay. I would never forgive myself if something happened.

"Ok Karter, we're going to wheel you down to the operating room and help you get set up for baby's arrival. Do you have any questions?"

"No, ma'am." I answered quickly and laid back in the bed. As excited as I was to meet my little prince, I wasn't ready for him to come just yet.

Chapter Twenty-Eight

Dezmund "Dez"

I paced the floor of the hospital, waiting for them to tell me I could go into the room with Karter. She was getting prepped for this C-section, and I was scared as fuck. Lil' man was supposed to be in there for a few more weeks. Karter was blaming herself for him having to come early, but I really didn't blame her. I was pissed that she kept it away from me that she was in pain, but that was it.

"Mr. Wright, you can come in now," this little black nurse said, and I almost pushed her ass out my way. When I walked in, they lead me to a stool that was at the head of the bed. Karter was looking scared, and I kissed her lips to try to calm her down.

"Ok, I'm starting now; you're going to feel some tugging and pressure, but it's normal. Just remember to keep breathing." I tried to look over the sheet they had up, but I couldn't see shit. "Loooottts of pressure." Karter's face was balled up, and I ain't know if I should go help or what I should do. My thoughts were going a mile a minute, until I heard, "He's here!"

"Is he ok? I don't hear him, why isn't he crying? Dez, go check on him!" I jumped up out my seat, and the nurses urged me to stay above the sheet. I was going to fight to see my baby, then I heard his little screams and felt a huge weight lifted off me. I watched the corner they took him to, and watched as they poked and probed all over him before they wrapped him in a blanket and walked over to us with him.

"Congrats, mommy and daddy; he's four pounds, eight ounces. He had to go to the NICU to get further checked, but so far, so good." I sat back in my seat, and she handed him to me. He was so tiny, I was scared that I was going to drop him.

"Let me see him, Dez."

"I can't move, Karter. I don't wanna break him or nothing." Everybody in the room laughed, and I looked around tryna see what the hell was so funny. After Karter got to see him, they put him in the little clear baby bed, and I followed them out the door. I took a few pictures on my phone and followed them to the NICU before I went to the waiting room, where the family was waiting.

"Are they ok? Is he here?" Melodee was the first person to rush me, and I handed her my phone. Ma and

Karter's mom gathered around Melodee, and were cooing at the picture of Junior.

"Congrats, big bro. I can't believe you somebody's pappy," Destini joked and handed me a cigar.

"Thanks, man. I can't believe it either. That shit was nerve wrecking, for real."

I waited in the family waiting room, until they came to tell me that Karter was in her recovery room. Everyone came to tell Karter congratulations, and promised to come back the next day after she got some rest.

"I'll bring you some clothes and shit, bro. Hit me up if you need me sooner." I dapped Dame up, and everyone left. Karter looked exhausted, and I knew it was from all of the drugs they pumped her up with.

I opened the let-out couch and got comfortable while Karter rested. I stayed up all night, looking at the picture of my son. Dezmund Edward Wright Jr just completed me, for real.

***

After being in the hospital for eight days, Karter and DJ were finally home. Karter could've been came home, but she refused to leave without him, and I wasn't going home by my damn self. Melodee and our moms got DJ's room together, and I was grateful for them three because it would've been a mess in here.

"How you feeling, baby?" I asked Karter as she tried to get comfortable in the bed.

"This shit still hurt like hell. I coughed earlier, and I swear I just wanted to die; it hurt soooo bad, bae. I didn't know about having more kids; this was too much."

"We'll revisit this conversation again next year." She looked at me like I lost my mind, and I laughed. "You feel like company today?"

"Not really, I just want to sleep while he's sleeping, with no interruptions. Tell everybody they can stop by tomorrow."

"Ok Queen, you rest. I'm about to go shower." I went to take a shower and wash the smell of hospital off me and when I came back to the room, Karter was knocked out with her mouth open. When I got dressed, I walked next door to DJ's room, and I saw he was just up looking around. I picked him up, and he was pecking away at my chest, like he was a chicken.

"I ain't yo' mama, dude. Let's go wake her up and whip those titties out. I'll let you borrow 'em for now, but you only got a couple months before I take 'em back... them belong to daddy, remember that." He just stared up at me with those big, eager eyes he got from his mother. He was the perfect blend of the both of us. He had my high yellow complexion, big pink lips, and head full of black curly hair, but he had Karter's doe eyes and little button nose. This lil' nigga was perfect, man. Don't tell Karter I called him that; she'll spazz.

I got in the bed and laid against the plush headboard. I tapped Karter on the butt, and she stirred a little and opened one eye. "Did you wake him up?"

"Nah man, he was looking at me when I check on him, and he was tryna milk me and shit. He need a nipple or something."

"Can you at least TRY to filter your mouth a little bit, please?"

"What I say? Nipple?"

"Dezmund!" she fussed, sitting up in the bed and taking DJ from me. He was swinging and having a fit when Karter lifted her shirt, and shit, the way her breast was looking, I wanted to suck on them bitches too.

When DJ was fed, burped, and changed, Karter gave him back to me, and she went to take a shower. This family man shit was going to be a breeze.

Chapter Twenty-Nine

Melodee

Six months later...

"That is the one! Yaaasss, you better slay them hoes!" Karter gassed me up as I tried on my third wedding dress. Dame and I decided on Jamaica for our destination wedding, and I couldn't wait to get on the islands.

"You said that to every dress, Karter. I'm started to think you lying."

"Noooo, I'm serious, that one is it." I twirled in the mirror, and I think I agreed with her. The dress I had on was a peach color, and it was tea length with a bateau lace neckline.

"Ok, I'll take it." I turned to the saleswoman, and she smiled bright and start ringing this damn loud ass bell.

"Damn, if she would've woke my baby up, I was gon' slap her," Karter said, peeking in lil' Dez's car seat, but he was still sleeping peacefully. I went to change back into my clothes so I could pay for the dress and leave. We were set to leave for Jamaica later tonight, and this was the last thing I needed to get.

"Are you nervous?" Karter asked as we walked to the car.

"About what?"

"Getting married, fool."

"I mean, a little bit, but I love him so I know I ain't making a mistake. Plus, Dame know ain't gon' be no divorce and shit. If he messes up, he's dead— period."

"You can't just kill people, Melodee."

"Why not?"

"I'm not even going to give you the satisfaction of answering that."

"Because you can't give me a good enough reason." Karter locked DJ's car seat in, and I put the stroller in the trunk before getting in the driver's seat. I drove to drop them off first, and I helped Karter get in the house. She was keeping my dress so nosey ass Damien wouldn't see it, and I was thankful for that.

"Thanks again, boo. I'll see you later, try to get some rest." I hugged her and kissed DJ on the forehead.

"I'll try, if your godson acts right."

I left and drove home. Dame must've still been out getting his hair cut and shit because his truck was gone.

Before I decided to take a nap, I checked my suitcases and made sure I had everything I wanted. We were staying in Jamaica for a week for our honeymoon, and I knew it was gon' be lit. Dame talked me into getting my birth control taken out because he was having baby fever. At first, I thought he was on that glass dick, but he was dead ass serious. I only agreed because he said he'd buy my Ghost I wanted as a push present. I just knew if he was lying, I was gon' be pushing that baby right back up there where it came from.

Thinking about my wedding, it kind of fucked with me that I didn't have my father to walk me down the aisle, but it was cool. After Dame sleeped his ass at his retirement party, I know he wasn't going nowhere near him, ever.

After I showered, I went right to sleep and didn't wake up until I felt Dame shaking the shit outta me.

"What the hell, Damien? You gon' give me fuckin' brain damage, shakin' me up and shit."

"Yo' ass sleep like you be hibernating, I had to do that. I got the truck loaded; it's time to go, baby."

I groaned and rolled out the bed. Looking over at the clock, it was three o'clock in the morning. It was about a five-hour flight to Montego Bay, Jamaica where the wedding was, and we wanted to be there early so we had more than enough time to be settled before the rehearsal dinner.

Once I threw my sweats on and slid my feet into my slides, we were out the door. When we got to the airstrip, I saw everybody boarding the plane. This was my second time on their private plane, and I was still in awe.

"Hey y'all, bye y'all. I'm going back to sleep." I got comfortable in the seat, and I think I was asleep before the plane took off.

***

Our rehearsal dinner wasn't even really a rehearsal dinner, because we didn't rehearse shit. We literally just ate and talked about what we were doing that night. Everyone

249

(except Ma) agreed to go to the club, so after we ate, we got changed and met outside at the cars. The clubs out here weren't like the ones back in the States. I was feelin' the fuck outta this music, and I was getting drunk as hell drinking this rum all night. Karter was dancing and shaking her ass on Dez, and I just knew she got pregnant. Even Destini had her a thick bitch in the club winding on her. Speaking of Destini, when she told me what that bitch Jakira did, I had her take me over there and whooped her ass all over her front lawn. I ride or die for mine, and if you hurt somebody I love, then I was gon' hurt you. JaKolby was mad and acted like he wanted to do something, but I guess he remembered who my man was and got over it real quick.

"Ay, I gotta fuck you real good one more time before we get married," Dame spoke in my ear, and he was slurring a little. I smelled the alcohol on his breath, so I knew he was fucked up. I think the only person who wasn't drinking was Karter because she was breastfeeding, and nobody was about to babysit Karter's baby ass when she got drunk.

"That sound good to me, but I thought it was bad luck or something?"

"Fuck that luck, I need some pussy." I laughed and moved my hips to the beat of the song. Dame was holding on for dear life, and he kept trying to slide his hands in my shorts.

"You wanna go relive the first night we met?"

"Hell yeah!" He grabbed my hand and pulled me toward the bathroom. Luckily, it was empty, so we rushed in and locked the door behind us. "Hurry up and take that shit off." I took my shorts off, and Dame grabbed me up swiftly, and it was like his rock hard member was a magnet the way it went to my tunnel.

"Ssssss, shiiiiit." We both moaned out together as he entered me slowly. I was pinned against the wall, and I was praying his drunk ass didn't drop me on this floor.

"Damn, this gon' be my pussy forever, huh?" My mouth was hanging open as Dame filled me up.

"Yeessssss, daddy, it's all yooouurrrrssss, fuck!" Dame grabbed my waist and was slammin' me down on his penis. People were banging on the door, so I know he was trying to get his nut so we could go.

"Fuck! You gon' cum with me, Mel? Let me feel like gushy shit, Mel."

"Ahhh!" He spoke the magic words and the floodgates opened, and I was cumming all over his manhood. When he growled in my ear, I knew he was nutting, and I felt him pulsating inside of me.

"Who is in here?! I have to use the bathroom!" somebody screamed with her voice dripping with irritation, but I didn't gave a damn because I was recovering from that orgasm… who could be mad after that?

We got cleaned up, put our clothes back on, and left out the bathroom. There was a dark-skinned chick standing outside of the door with her arms crossed, and we just walked past her and went back to the area where our people were.

"Y'all some nasty motherfuckas," Destini said as we made it to the section, and I sat down next to her.

"We sho is some nasty motherfuckers, because I definitely just blessed their bathroom."

I looked over at Dame, and he went right back to the bottle and was drinking. I already knew he was gon' want to finish what we started, and I was all ready for him. I could definitely get used to this for the rest of my life.

Epilogue

The Big Day

First time I look into your eyes, I saw heaven – oh-heaven, in your eyes

Everything I did before you, wasn't worth my time

It should have been you, you all the time

I do anything and everything, to please you.

Brian McKnight's 'Love of My Life' was blaring through the speakers as Melodee made her way down the aisle to her awaiting groom. Both were full of nerves, but ready for what was about to happen. The last two years that Dame and Melodee had been together had been everything but a cakewalk, but they stuck it out and made it work together.

The closer she got to the altar, the more Dame's heart was pounding out of his chest. His bride to be was beautiful, and he was trying to hold his tears in, because he knew his brother and sister wouldn't let him live it down.

Seeing Dame dressed in his cream linen suit, Melodee licked her lips at how sexy he was. Once Melodee took her spot in front of Dame, the officiant started the ceremony.

"Welcome, family, friends, and loved ones. We gather here today, to celebrate the union of Damien and Melodee. You come here to share in this formal commitment they make to one another, to offer your love and support so that Damien and Melodee can start their married life together surrounded by the people dearest and most important to them." The officiant went on to explain what marriage is, and what it means to be married. As he spoke, Dame and Melodee stared lovingly into each other's eyes.

"We've come to the point of your ceremony where you're going to say your vows to one another. But, before you do that, just remember that love— which is rooted in faith, trust, and acceptance— is the foundation of an abiding relationship. No other ties are more sacred than those you now assume. Please now read the vows you have written for each other." He handed the mic over the Melodee, and she cleared her throat before she spoke.

"Damien… I want to start off by telling you how much I love you, and how grateful I am to have you in my life. Thank you for never giving up on me, even when I know I was driving you crazy. You are truly my best friend, and I'm lucky to have you in my life. You never ju—" Melodee got choked up on her words and stopped to get herself together before she continued. "You never judged me because of my past, you're always there to pick me up when I'm down and push me when I want to give up. And, as long as I may live, I promise to be all of that plus more for you." When she finished her vows, she was in tears, and Karter had to give her some tissue to wipe her eyes. It was now Dame's turn, and his hand was shaking as he held the mic in one hand, and Melodee's hand in the other.

"Melodee… you know I ain't good at this type of sh— stuff, but Imma try for you. Before I met you, I never even thought of myself as a relationship type; it just wasn't me. But, you came along, and I knew I never wanted anybody else. Yeah, you crazy as hell, but so am I; that's why we work." Everyone laughed at him as he continued. "I promise to love you, and stay true to you, even when you're old and gray. You're my best friend, and I can't imagine myself without you." His voice was breaking, and a tear rolled slowly down his cheek. Melodee's eyes got big, and there wasn't a dry eye on the beach. "Here, I'm done."

Leave it to Dame to mess up the romantic moment, Melodee thought as she dried her eyes again.

The rings were exchanged, and Dame didn't wait until the officiant told him to kiss his wife before he grabbed her and kissed her so deep, her knees got weak.

"Well, I now present to you, the newly married couple, Mr. and Mrs. Damien Wright."

All their family was cheering and clapping as the couple turned around to face them. This was one of the happiest days of Melodee and Damien's life, and they were happy to spend it with one another.

Melodee looked up at her husband, and knew she made the right choice as she said, "I love you King, this is forever."

"I love you more, Queen. You already know we're in this for life."

The End... maybe :)

Keep reading to check out a sneak peek for one of my upcoming releases!!

Draft Day

Dejae

"I am here, live, in the Oracle Arena as we, the fans, wait to see who's going to be added to our family this year. And... it looks like the commissioner of the NBA, Adam Silver, is ready. Let's take a look." Everyone in the packed arena turned toward the giant screen as we watched the draft on television.

"With the first pick in the 2017 NBA draft, the Philadelphia 76ers select.... Lionel Kidd from the University of Washington."

I tried to focus on what was going on, but my phone kept buzzing in my pocket. I stepped away from the crowd and checked to see there was a bunch of texts and missed calls from my fiancé, Jotti. I hurriedly called him back before they got to Golden State's pick.

"What the hell are you calling so much for, Jotti? What's wrong?"

"I'm so sorry, Dej. I swear, it was only once, I know you're gonna flip, but we can work through this." My heart dropped listening to him say sorry, and I knew that only meant he cheated again.

"What did you do, Jotti?"

"She... she got pregnant, Dej."

You know that feeling you get in your stomach when your heart's broken? It's like all the butterflies just died, and you feel empty inside. That's what I felt as I stared down at the phone in my hand.

Pregnant? How the fuck does somebody just get pregnant?

"Dej, baby are you still there?"

"I have to go."

I hung up and stuffed the cellphone back in my pocket. As I walked back out to the camera crew, I shook off any sad emotion I had and planted a big fake smile on as the commissioner made the next announcement.

"With the fifth pick in the 2017 NBA draft, the Golden State Warriors select Saieed Bishop from the University of California, Los Angeles."

The crowd went wild as Adam Silver announced the next player to join the Warriors team. The cameraman did a countdown as I got ready to go live again.

"Well, there you have it, the Warriors have picked Saieed Bishop. He attended the UCLA, where he made quite a name for himself, averaging 14.8 points per game and 8.7 rebounds. We can definitely use him on the team. I can't wait to see how Steve is going to use his greatness to match with the rest of the team. We're going to hear a word from Mike, who is live at the Barclays Centers in Brooklyn. Mike, what's it looking like over there?"

The camera man signaled that I was off air, and I felt like I couldn't breathe.

"You ok, Dejae?" one of my colleagues asked as I gulped down a bottle of water to stop myself from crying. This was a trick my mama taught me a very long time ago. She knew that in this industry, where you rarely saw women, you had to have tough skin.

"No, actually, I'm feeling a bit under the weather. I think I ate some bad sushi or something earlier. Do you mind covering for me?"

"Yeah, go ahead. I hope you feel better, I'll see you later."

I thanked him and walked as fast as I could out of the arena, and to my car.

When I started the car, I pulled off and sped to Jotti's, which was about 45 minutes from the arena.

His Maserati was parked in the driveway, so I knew he was home. Before I even got out the car, I took my pumps off and threw them in the passenger seat so I could move quicker.

I made it to his front door and banged on the glass door. I could've used my key, but it was deep in my purse, and I ain't have time for all of that.

"Dej—"

Wap!

I smacked him so hard across his face, my hand was stinging. "How fucking dare you, Jotti, after everything?!"

"Come inside before someone hear you out here."

"I DON'T GIVE A FUCK!!" He snatched me in the house and closed the door behind me.

Me and Jotti had been together for five years. He was a few years older than me, but that's what I liked about him. But, he'd cheated so many times, and even though I knew I deserved more, I just didn't want to leave him and explain to everyone how my fiancé couldn't keep his dick in his pants.

"Who is it this time, Jotti?"

"Candance." He put his head down and at that moment, I wish I had a bat or a gun, because his life would be over.

Let me give y'all a little insight on who Candance is. She's dumbass's assistant down at his PR firm. He's in the right fucking business, because so far, none of his damn cheating has come up anywhere. But you can't hide a whole life.

"For years, YEARS, you told me, 'oh don't worry about her, baby, it's just business'." I mocked that stupid ass high pitched voice he gets when his ass is lying.

"I was... I didn't mean to... it was one time and I was drunk, and I swear it'll never happen again."

"Who's to say it was only one time? For all I know, it was a hundred fucking times." I swear, if I was a couple shades lighter, my skin would probably be red with how pissed I was.

"I'm sorry."

"Yeah, you are… real fucking sorry. I can't do this. I stuck by the cheating, I believe you every time you said it was the last time, but a baby? You want me to forgive a baby?" I took a breath to wipe the tears from my eyes and looked up at him.

"I can't forgive that. I'm done, Jotti." I took my engagement ring off and put it on the table that was close to me.

Everything in my heart was telling me to try my luck and punch him in his damn mouth, but Mama and Daddy ain't raise no fool. I walked out the door and ran down to my car, with Jotti calling for me to come back. Hopping in my car, I sped off and went right to the interstate.

I couldn't stop the tears that fell from my eyes as I drove down the interstate. I didn't have a destination; I was just driving.

My phone was ringing, and I saw best friend, Rayven's, name pop up on the screen. I wiped my tears and put my phone on the deck before I answered.

"Hey boo, what you doing?"

"Just left from Barclays. I told Semaj I was only staying until his brother was announced, and I was bouncing. My feet are killing me, and this baby ain't making it no better. What you doing, though?"

"Driving."

"Answer the Facetime. Are you crying? What's wrong, boo?"

"Me and Jotti just broke up."

"Aaww, why? I loved y'all together." I never told anyone about all Jotti's cheating, because the shit was embarrassing. Then, it's not like I left him... until now.

"He's been cheating, and now he had the nerve to get the bitch pregnant."

"That stupid bastard. I'm so glad we moving out there. We can jump him after I have this baby."

Hearing that, I perked up real fast. "You moving back?"

264

"Yeah, Semaj is Saieed's manager, so we're moving back, baybeeeeee. It's going to be in a few months after I have this baby, but now, I have the green light to go house shopping."

"I'm so happy, I can't wait. But, I just got home. I need to unwind and think of a lie to tell my boss."

"Ok boo, call me if you need me."

I hung up the phone and had to take a deep breath before I got out car.

"Be strong enough to let go, and wise enough to wait for what you deserve." -Unknown

Coming Soon...

Let's Chat!

Facebook: AJ Dix
Instagram: Ashley_Jovan

Follow my Facebook group 'AJs Readers Group' for sneak peeks, discussions and giveaways!

More great reads from A.J:

Shorty Fell in Love With a Dope Boy: 1 & 2

In Love With The King of Chicago

He Want a Lil' Baby That's Gone Listen: Dynasti & Smoove

Have You Grabbed This Yet?
#Free With Kindle Unlimited!

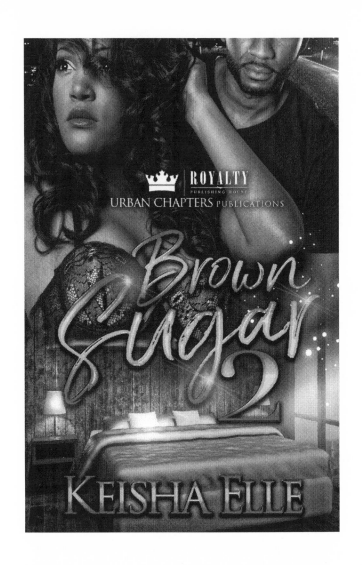

Made in the USA
Monee, IL
06 November 2019